Dr Jekyll and Mr Hollins

Henry stared into his father's face. "Hey, Dad!" he said, in puzzled tones. "Did you shave this morning?"

"Of course I did!" replied Albert, almost in a growl.

"But your face – it's . . . it's going all hairy, Dad! All hairy and sort of wrinkled!"

"Don't talk daft, lad!" replied Albert hoarsely.

But, putting his hands up to his cheeks, he discovered that what Henry had told him was true. The face that he had shaved only a couple of hours before was now covered in bristly hair!

"What's happened to me?" he cried.

Willis Hall

Dr Jekyll and Mr Hollins

Illustrated by Maggie Ling

Lions
An Imprint of HarperCollinsPublishers

First published in Great Britain by
The Bodley Head 1988
First published in Young Lions 1991

Young Lions is an imprint of
the Children's Division, part of
HarperCollins Publishers Ltd,
77–85 Fulham Palace Road, Hammersmith,
London W6 8JB

ISBN 0 00 674060-X

Set in Garamond

Printed and bound in Great Britain by
HarperCollins Manufacturing, Glasgow

1

"Albert dear," said Emily Hollins across the break-fast table to her husband, "I wonder if I might beg a small favour of you?"

"What's that?"

Unnoticed by Emily, Albert raised his eyebrows nervously at their eleven-year-old son, Henry, giving him a *What's-your-mother-up-to-this-time?* look. Albert Hollins had good reason to be anxious. Whenever Emily begged a "very small favour" of him, it usually turned into something rather big.

"That shirt you're wearing," said Emily.

"It's got a button missing," replied Albert quickly, thinking this must be what was worrying Emily. He was eager to get out of the house, into his car and off to his job in the office at the local garden gnome factory.

"Yes, dear, I *know* it's got a button missing. And I happen to know just where that button is – it's in the cat's basket – though what it's doing in the cat's basket, I can't imagine. But going back to the shirt, Albert – I wonder if you'd mind slipping it off for me?"

"I can manage without the button, actually," said Albert, gulping his tea. If he got to the garden gnome factory early enough, there was usually a cup of instant coffee to be had with the office cleaners. "I've slipped a safety pin through the cuff and, provided Mr Wormald doesn't ask me to take my coat off and stack some crates of fishing gnomes this morning, I don't think anyone's going to notice." He glanced at his watch. "Anyway, Emily, it's time I was on my way." If he got to the office *very* early there was sometimes a chocolate biscuit going spare as well.

But Emily was not to be put off so easily.

"I'm not concerned about the missing button, Albert," she said. "Not this morning. Just do as I say, dear, and slip your shirt off."

"What? Here? Now? At the breakfast table?" Albert winked at Henry. "Whatever *for*?" he said.

"Of course not here!" Emily was in no mood for joking. "Upstairs. Put it in the laundry basket and take a clean one out of the airing cupboard."

"I haven't *got* a clean one!"

"Yes, you have, Albert – there's that nice summery one with all the palm trees on it and HOLLYWOOD written across the back."

"I can hardly sit in the office at Garden Gnomes, doing a responsible job of work, with HOLLYWOOD stamped across my back for one and all to see!"

"But no one will see it, will they, dear? Not if you keep your jacket on like you said. In any case, it's not the only shirt you possess – there are plenty of clean ones in your drawer if you'll only *look* for them."

"But this one *is* clean," moaned Albert, with visions of both the chocolate biscuit *and* the cup of instant coffee disappearing in a cloud of smoke.

"It doesn't look very clean to me, Albert," said Emily with a sniff. "I'd say it looks rather grubby."

"It's spotless, Emily!" Albert insisted. Turning to his son, he added, "How does it look to you, Henry?"

Henry Hollins gave a non-committal grunt and stared into the bowl of Wheatie Snax he was having for breakfast.

Whenever Emily and Albert disagreed and called upon their son to arbitrate, Henry always tried to sound non-committal. Otherwise, he found himself having to take sides. But it was not going to be easy to keep out of things that morning. Emily was staring hard at her son.

"That pullover you're wearing, Henry, looks to me as if it could do with going in the washer," his mother said.

"But I only put it on this morning, Mum," protested Henry.

"Never mind, dear. When your father goes upstairs to change his shirt, you go along with him and put on a nice clean pullover."

"But, Mum—"

"No 'buts', Henry," said Emily, comfortably, "Mother knows best."

Albert and Henry looked at one another hopelessly.

"My word!" Emily went on. "Those kitchen curtains look as if they need to be taken down and given a real good seeing to."

"Emily!" said Albert, keenly. "You're up to something, aren't you?"

"*Me*? Up to something?" Emily's voice was so full of innocence it was obvious that innocent was the last thing that she was.

"Emily," said Albert, "those kitchen curtains were taken down only last week, put in the machine and given 'a real good seeing to' then – and I know that for certain because I spent most of Sunday evening – when I could have been watching snooker on the telly – trying to thread the blessed string back through them! What *are* you up to?"

"When, dear?"

"*Now*!"

"Do you mean this morning, Albert?" Emily sounded even more innocent than before. "Why, I'm going to put your shirt, Henry's pullover and the kitchen curtains in the washing machine – and then I might just hand-wash the cat's blanket."

"What's going on?" demanded Albert, who now knew that his wife *was* up to something.

"Oh – very well. I was hoping to keep it from you for another day or two, but if you insist on being told . . ."

"I do."

"I do too," said Henry.

Emily smiled a happy little smile and hugged herself as she savoured the last few precious moments of having a secret. She looked first at Albert, then at Henry.

"I only need to collect one more and we've got enough to go on a Diamond-Days Weekend," she said, excitedly, and added, "Isn't it wonderful?"

Albert and Henry looked at her blankly.

"Collect one more what?" asked Albert.

"What's a Diamond-Days Weekend?" asked Henry.

"Don't either of you read the newspapers?"

"Only the football page," said Henry.

"Don't either of you watch the commercials on the telly?"

"Very rarely," said Albert, sternly. "I'm usually

9

kept far too busy these days – trying to thread string through curtains."

"I've only got to collect one more packet top from Soapy Suds washing-powder cartons to go on a Diamond-Days Weekend holiday!"

"Great, Mum!" said Henry, enthusiastically.

But Albert was not quite so pleased.

"I should have known it!" he cried. "I should have recognized the signs. Last week when you washed the chair covers twice! The reason why there's always washing on the line, seven days a week, day and night. The fact that I've had twelve pairs of socks laid out for me this week – I was beginning to think that I'd got three feet!" Albert paused, folded his arms, narrowed his eyes and frowned at his wife across the table. "Emily," he said, "how long has this been going on?"

"Not long."

"*How* long?"

"It's only been in these last few weeks that I've speeded up things," explained Emily in a small apologetic voice. "Only since I've been getting near my target."

"And what exactly was your target?"

"Three thousand five hundred packet tops," said Emily, in an even smaller voice.

"Three thousand five hundred!" howled Albert.

"Wow," said Henry.

"But just think of it, dear," said Emily. "We've got three thousand four hundred and ninety-nine."

Albert did not seem to be impressed.

"Are you telling me," he said, "that we've gone through three thousand five hundred packets of Soapy Suds washing powder?"

"Not quite, Dad," Henry put in, "we've still got one more to go."

"Don't interrupt me, son," said his father, coldly. "Three thousand five hundred! The mind boggles! Why, it's enough soap powder, is that, to wash a First Division soccer club's mucky strip for years and years! It's enough soap powder to keep every chimney sweep in the Common Market spotless for a lifetime!"

"But we've done it now, Albert!" cried Emily and, as she spoke, she produced a glossy leaflet from her handbag. "We've earned ourselves a Diamond-Days Weekend! *Each day as precious as a diamond in your life.*' That's what it says in here."

Albert slowly blew out a long breath through his closed teeth and shook his head. "And what, exactly, are we letting ourselves in for this time?" he said. "This family has never been on holiday yet, Emily, without getting into bother."*

*To discover exactly what kind of bother the Hollins family has previously encountered, read: *The Last Vampire; The Inflatable Shop* and *Dragon Days*.

"That's true, Mum," agreed Henry.

Emily gave a firm shake of her head. "Not this time," she said. "This time we've dropped in lucky. Two nights in a de luxe hotel of our choice, with en suite bathroom or shower – all three of us. With tea-making facilities and colour telly in every room. Full board from our three-star arrival on Friday night until our departure on Sunday afternoon – preceded by a full three-course Sunday lunch inclusive of coffee and after-dinner mints. *And* free travel, there and back, on a fully air-conditioned luxury coach with resident hostess, mid-morning coffee and loo."

Albert glanced at his watch again. He was going to be late for work. Fred Tompkins would be stamping his feet outside the office door now – waiting for the paint-shop keys so that he could get inside and start mixing the red gloss paint for the gnome hats. Even so, Albert had to admit to himself, this latest jaunt of Emily's did sound intriguing. Perhaps he could give himself just a couple more minutes . . .

"And where are we going on this wild weekend?" said Albert.

"Why – wherever we desire," replied Emily. "The choice is up to us entirely."

"Anywhere?" asked Henry, excitedly. "Can we go to Los Angeles, Mum? To *Disneyland*?"

"Well, not quite that far, Henry."

"Be sensible, son," said Albert. "You can't get to Disneyland and back in one weekend – not in a coach, you can't, and that *is* a fact." He paused and then smiled as a thought occurred to him. "Hey!" he cried, clapping his hands together. "We might just manage the South of France though, if the coach driver puts his foot down! Whoops-a-Daisy! Riviera, here we come!"

"I don't think we could quite get there either, Albert," said Emily, doubtfully. "I think the rules do restrict us to these shores. I thought we might plump for London – it looks very nice in the brochure – 'Wake up to a panoramic view of England's capital,' it says."

"Terrific, Mum!" cried Henry. "There's the Chamber of Horrors, there's the Tower of London, there's the London Dungeon – what do you think, Dad?"

"I suppose so," said Albert, nodding. "I suppose it sounds all right. If I'm not to be allowed to dabble my tootsies in the Mediterranean – go hobnobbing with the rich and famous in Nice or Cannes – I suppose London's quite acceptable. And when might we look forward to this little trip, Emily? When will it be 'all systems go'?"

"Why – just as soon as I get through this last economy packet of Soapy Suds washing powder. Next weekend, I thought we might aim for.

Now – will you get yourselves upstairs, the pair of you, and let me have that shirt and pullover so I can get the washing machine going?"

Henry Hollins and his father, both realizing now that a weekend trip to London depended entirely on Emily using up the washing powder, got up from the breakfast table and headed, with all speed, for the bedroom stairs.

> "It's a long way to Piccadilly,
> It's a long way, we know.
> It's a long way to Piccadilly,
> Down the motorway we'll go!"

The passengers sang cheerfully on the luxury coach as it zoomed down the motorway, heading towards London. There were a couple of hours still to go before they were due to arrive at their destination and, to pass the time, a sing-song had been organized.

"I wish it was going to be two weeks instead of two days," whispered Albert to his wife and son. "Just think of it – no more garden gnomes to be despatched for an entire fortnight!"

The coach was not *quite* full and the Hollins family had managed to acquire the whole of the back seat for themselves.

"Oh, I don't know so much," said Emily, happily.

"Two whole days in London will suit me very nicely, thank you very much."

"And me," said Henry. "Just so long as we get to the Chamber of Horrors and the London Dungeon."

"Good afternoon!" said the pleasant-faced young woman in a smart red blazer with a gold wire badge on its pocket. The young woman had made her way over to the rear of the coach and was standing over the Hollins family, smiling down at them. "It *is* Mr and Mrs Hollins, isn't it?"

"It is indeed," replied Emily. "This is our son, Henry."

"Hello," said Henry, smiling up at the newcomer.

"Hi!" said the young woman. "I'm Debbie, your in-coach hostess."

"Very pleased to meet you, I'm sure," said Albert.

"Only I like to make myself known to all my passengers," said Debbie, giving them a broad smile. "You're the family on the Diamond-Days three-star Weekend, aren't you? Courtesy of Soapy Suds washing powder?"

"That's us," said Albert.

"You're the very first winners of that particular prize I've ever had on board," said Debbie, her eyes widening. "Three thousand five hundred packet tops you had to collect, wasn't it? My word, I *am* impressed – it must have taken some doing."

"Ask Emily," said Albert Hollins, proudly. "She's the one responsible."

Emily Hollins shrugged, modestly. "Oh, I mustn't take *all* the credit," she said. "It was my washing machine that had to bear most of the work."

"Well, I hope you enjoy your weekend – all three of you," said Debbie. "You certainly deserve it. Where will you be staying in London, if you don't mind my asking? Which was the first-class three-star hotel of your choice?"

"Oooh!" said Emily, her forehead wrinkling as she thought hard. "What's it called now? Come on, Albert, you ought to know – you picked it out of the brochure."

"I picked it out, yes," admitted Albert, with

16

a shake of his head. "But I'm blowed if I can remember its name."

"The Emilion," said Henry.

"The Emilion in Bayswater?" Debbie's eyes opened even wider.

All three members of the Hollins family nodded their heads.

"You're never!" gasped the in-coach hostess.

"We are," said Emily.

"Well! Isn't it a small world! I'm booked in there myself – it's my weekend off."

"Are you really?" exclaimed Emily, pleased and surprised.

"We'll look forward to bumping into you, per-haps?" said Albert.

"I hope so," said Debbie, enthusiastically. "Any-way I can't stop now – I'm supposed to keep this lot entertained—" She glanced over her shoulder at the rest of her charges who were now all sitting silently in their seats. "Come on, miseries!" she called out at them. "What's happened to the sing-song? I hope you've not all run out of puff? We're not in London yet, you know – nowhere near! – we've only just passed Watford Gap! Sing up!"

Spurred on by their hostess, the coach passengers struck up another chorus of song as the luxury vehicle continued smoothly on its course along the motorway.

Henry Hollins, his mother, Emily, and his father, Albert, joined in and sang along happily with their fellow passengers.

The Hollins family might not, perhaps, have been quite so carefree, had they known of the strange and eventful adventure that was waiting for them at the end of their journey.

2

"And over here, sir and madam," said the smart brown-uniformed porter with the neatly trimmed moustache, "is your early morning tea-making equipment – should you be desirous of an early morning cup of tea, that is—"

"Oooh!" said Emily, interrupting him. "I like my early morning cup of tea – I'm not properly awake until I've got a cup of tea inside me."

"Quite so, madam," said the porter, a little stiffly. He was eager to point out to the new guests all the luxurious delights that the Hotel Emilion had to offer and was a little peeved at being interrupted.

"And here's your television set," he continued, "with bedside fingertip control – right next to your trouser press with automatic switch-off setting."

"That'll come in useful," said Albert, approvingly.

"I hope so, sir," said the hotel porter.

Turning to Henry, who was sitting on the bed

19

swinging his legs, he added, "And your room, young man, is exactly the same and right next door – here's the key."

"Thanks very much," said Henry.

"Well, sir and madam," said the porter, "if there's nothing else you might be wanting now, I'll leave you all to settle in."

"I can't think of anything, off the cuff," said Albert.

The porter shuffled his feet on the bedroom's thick orange carpet and scratched his left ear, but made no attempt to leave.

Albert Hollins, suddenly realizing what was wanted, stuck his hand inside his trouser pocket and pulled out a fistful of coins. He selected a fifty-pence piece and pressed it into the porter's open hand.

"Oh, thank *you*, sir!" said the porter in pretended surprise, looking down at the coin in his palm as if it was the very last thing in the world he expected to find there. "May I say that I hope you enjoy your Diamond-Days Weekend with us – and that the Hotel Emilion fulfils your every expectation! My name is Perkins, you'll find me constantly in attendance at the porter's desk in the entrance hall – I am at your beck and call – you are required only to pick up that telephone." With which, he saluted smartly, turned and strode out.

Emily Hollins looked at the door through which Perkins had left. "He seemed a very helpful sort of chap," she said. "I must say, I'm quite impressed with our weekend so far – what do you two say?"

"Seems great to me," said Henry, who was still sitting on the end of the bed.

"It'll do, I'm sure," said Albert. But he frowned as he peered down into the basement area through the curtained window. "I can't say I'm all that impressed with the view though – three overflowing dustbins up against a concrete wall are not exactly *my* idea of a panoramic picture of London town!"

"I'm sure it looks much nicer when the dustbin-men have been, dear," said Emily, brightly. "In any case, it's not as if we were going to spend our entire weekend staring out into the basement yard – we've only got two days and we've all the sights to see!"

"What are we going to do first, Mum?" asked Henry eagerly, slipping his feet on to the floor.

"Well now, I can't speak for you two, but I do know what *I'm* going to do – and that's unpack for all three of us. Why don't you two go down and explore the hotel?"

"I'm not sure there's all that much to explore," said Albert, doubtfully. "What do you say, son?"

Henry shrugged. "Don't mind," he said.

"You might find out where they keep the dining room, for a kick-off," Emily pointed out. "We don't want to be caught short at breakfast-time tomorrow if we're at all pushed for time. And you might see if there are any postcards going spare at the reception desk – we'll need to post them off first thing tomorrow if we're sending any."

"Righty-ho," said Albert, moving towards the door. "Come on, Henry."

Albert had decided that it might be a good idea to get out of the bedroom anyway, while Emily was unpacking. When Emily Hollins unpacked a suitcase it was as if a small whirlwind was in the room. She would shoot from suitcase to drawer; from drawer to cupboard; from cupboard to wardrobe and from wardrobe back to suitcase almost, it seemed, at the speed of light – and woe betide any man, boy or beast that got in her path, as Albert, Henry and the Hollins cat had frequent cause to remember.

"There is one small favour you could do for me before you go," said Emily.

"What's that?"

"You might lift that big suitcase up on to that thing that suitcases go on."

"This suitcase, Emily?" asked Albert, putting both hands around the handle.

"If you wouldn't mind."

Albert Hollins jerked upwards on the handle with

both hands, but he had forgotten, for the moment, the weight of the suitcase and its contents.

"Oooh!" said Albert, clutching at the small of his back.

"What's up, Dad?" said Henry.

"It's nothing, Henry, it's just a little . . . *Ow!*" went Albert as his probing fingers found a tender spot.

"It isn't 'just a little' anything," observed Emily, with a worried frown. "*I'll* tell you what it is, Henry – it's your father's back trouble again. It's his garden gnome's disease."

Garden gnome's disease was a common complaint in the garden gnome factory where Albert Hollins worked. It was caused by constantly lifting garden gnomes and putting them into packing cases.

"It's not garden gnome's disease at all!" snapped Albert. "It's just a little . . . *Aaaagghhh!*"

"Don't argue with me, Albert," replied Emily. "It's my fault – I should never have asked you to lift that heavy suitcase."

"Really, Emily! Don't *fuss*!" said Albert. "I'll be as right as rain again in a couple of . . . *Oh!*"

"Have you got anything for it, Dad?" asked Henry, with some concern.

"He hasn't got anything for it, no," said Emily, sharply. "But he's going out to get something – and double-quick too!"

23

"I've told you, Emily, I shall be . . . *Ouch!*"

"We know very well what you'll be, Albert. You'll be 'Oooh-ing' and 'Oh-ing' and 'Ah-ing' all night long. You'll do as I say. You'll go down to that porter's desk, now, and see that nice Mr Perkins. You'll ask him how you go about seeing the hotel doctor."

"But, Emily . . ."

"No 'buts', Albert – this minute!"

"Yes, Emily . . . Ooooch!"

It took, in fact, all of five minutes for Albert and Henry to make their way down from the fourth floor to the brightly lit lobby – partly because they had to wait for the lift and partly because Albert's aching back slowed down their progress. They found Perkins behind his porter's desk, briskly sharpening a yellow pencil.

Perkins listened solemnly to Albert's question. He pondered for a while as he examined the sharp point he had shaped on the end of his pencil, then he shook his head.

"The hotel doctor, is it, sir?" asked Perkins. "Now there you do pose us a problem."

"Why's that?" said Albert, and added, "*Ouch!*" as he felt another twinge.

"It's Dad's back," explained Henry. "He's done something to it, lifting a heavy suitcase."

"Then he has my every sympathy, young man – I

know just how he feels," said Perkins, testing out his pencil-point on the unused snow-white blotting pad on his desk. Then, apparently satisfied with the pencil, he continued, "You should see some of the suitcases *I'm* asked to lug about. Suitcases; trunks; portmanteaux – there was a blooming great iron-bound chest on one never-to-be-forgotten occasion! There was! It belonged to an American lady – a Miss Gloria Hammerschraft who hailed from Pittsburgh. You may not believe this, both of you, but I humped that iron-bound chest down three separate flights of stairs, the lift being out of order on that particular occasion – yes, it was the winter of the big freeze-up, I remember it well—"

"Oooh—!" went Albert, as a sharp pain shot up his back as far as his left shoulder blade.

"Pardon me, sir?" said the porter. "Are you feeling all right?"

"Quite all right, thank you, Mr Perkins," groaned Albert. "At least, I *shall* be all right as soon as I get hold of some embrocation for my back."

"He needs to see the hotel doctor," said Henry.

"I'm sorry," said the porter, "I thought I'd explained all that already – yes, indeed, Mr Hollins, you do present us with a problem there!"

"Why?" asked Henry. "Hasn't the hotel got a doctor?"

25

Perkins put a hand to his mouth to hide a little laugh. "Forgive my amusement," he said. "But a hotel of this size without a doctor on instant call – why the very idea is unthinkable! The Hotel Emilion without a doctor! It's as unlikely as the QE2 without a captain on her bridge!"

"Where can we find him then?" asked Henry, giving his father an anxious glance as he let out yet another groan.

"As I say, young Hollins, we do have a slight crisis on our hands," said Perkins, tapping his pencil on the top of his desk. "Doctor Murchison, the Hotel Emilion's GP, is at home with a cold."

"The hotel doctor's off work with a cold?" said Albert, indignantly. "Can't he give himself something for it?"

"He's been unable to shift it," replied the porter, with a sigh. "Try as he might – it's been hanging over him for a fortnight. 'I know what I'm going to do, Perkins,' he said, because he speaks to me like that, sir, man to man, 'I know what I'm going to do, Perkins, I'm going to tuck myself up with a hot water bottle and not stir out of bed before Monday morning.'"

"Monday!" gasped Henry. "But it's only Friday evening now – and, besides, we're going home on Sunday afternoon!"

"At the risk of repeating myself, young man, we

do have a problem," said Perkins, again examining carefully the fine point on his pencil.

"Oooh!" went Albert as another twinge shot up his back, heading this time towards his *right* shoulder blade.

"Is it *very* painful, sir?" asked Perkins, sympathetically.

"Painful enough, Mr Perkins," groaned Albert. "Isn't there another doctor somewhere?"

"Perhaps there's another surgery outside the hotel but close by?" suggested Henry.

"No, no, no, no," said the porter, shaking his head, "I've been portering at the Hotel Emilion ever since it was opened and I can't recall— Hang on a tiny jiffy, there *is* a doctor's surgery!" he exclaimed and, in his excitement, he pressed his pencil down, hard, on his blotter, breaking off the point.

"Where is it?" asked Henry.

"Go out of the hotel, right? And then turn left."

"Right and then left," repeated Henry.

"Not right and left, young man – just left," said Perkins. "When I said 'right' that was just a figure of speech. Turn left, then left again – that'll take you off the main road – and about two hundred yards down the street you'll see a low archway on your right. Go through the archway and you'll find yourselves in a little cobbled courtyard – it's a strange old place, almost Dickensian in its way."

"A *cobbled* courtyard, did you say?" asked Albert.

"That's it, sir – you can't mistake it. A very old-fashioned area – there's even an old gas lamp – it's almost as if time had passed it by . . . But I'm willing to swear that there's a doctor's surgery – over on the far side. Not that I've ever had cause to use it – but it's been there donkey's years. There's a worn brass plate outside this old dark door – almost spooky . . ." The porter's voice trailed away as he frowned and contemplated the broken point on his pencil.

"Come on, Dad – we'll find it," urged Henry, setting off with all speed towards the hotel entrance.

Albert Hollins limped painfully after his son, one hand clutching the small of his back. "Slowly, Henry," he said, pulling a face. "Not too fast now!"

"Mind you don't walk past the archway," cautioned Perkins. "It's getting dark outside."

It *was* getting dark outside, as Henry Hollins and his father discovered as they came out of the hotel. It seemed even darker once they were off the main road, where the busy London traffic hurtled past, and in the quiet of the street that ran down the side of the hotel. They managed to find the archway without any difficulty.

Henry led the way and Albert limped after him

through the short dark passage, blackened with the grime of years, into the cobbled square. It was exactly as Perkins had described it to them: a strange forgotten place with a flickering gas lamp casting curious shadows into odd corners. It was as if they had entered a world of long ago. There were two gnarled trees set in the cobbles, their branches heavy with leaves that hung motionless in the still air. There was just a hint of fog.

"If you ask me," ventured Albert, nervously, "this is hardly the place for a doctor's surgery – it's too gloomy by half—"

"*Whoo-hoo*!"

"Good Lord above!" gasped Albert, with a shiver. "What on earth was that?"

"I . . . I think it was an owl, Dad," said Henry, feeling none too brave himself.

"An *owl*?" gulped Albert. "In the middle of London? It doesn't make sense!"

"It *is* an owl," replied Henry, pointing into the branches overhead. "It's sitting up there – I can see its eyes blinking."

Albert shivered again as his gaze followed Henry's pointing finger. He looked around the empty cobbled square and at the tall, dark, brooding buildings on all four sides.

"I'm not struck on this place, Henry," said Mr Hollins. "I'm not struck on it one little bit – let's go back to the hotel, eh? I wouldn't say 'no' to a glass of lager – and I'm sure you could manage a Coke if you tried?"

"Wait a minute, Dad," said Henry, peering through the gathering mist into the farthest corner of the square. "Perhaps Mr Perkins was right – there *is* a door with a brass plate by the side of it – I can just make it out in the gas-light."

"And that's another thing," mumbled Henry's dad. "Whoever heard of gas lamps in these enlightened times! Let's get out of here, son."

But Henry, summoning up his courage, had crossed to the gloomy building in the corner of the square and was peering hard at the lettering on the metal plaque.

"What does it say, son?" asked Mr Hollins who, deciding that there was safety in numbers, had limped to Henry's side.

"It's hard to tell in this light," said Henry, screwing up his eyes. "And the plate's all worn and dirty – I don't think anybody's polished it for yonks."

"*Whoo-hooo*!" went the owl again.

"My back is suddenly beginning to feel much better!" announced Albert. "Come *on*, Henry – your mother must be wondering what's become of us!"

"Just a minute, Dad. The moon's coming out

from behind that cloud – I think I should be able to read what it says—"

Sure enough, a moment later, the full moon began to steal out from behind a thick belt of cloud, touching the leaves on the trees with silver and bathing the cobbled square in a ghostly light.

Henry screwed up his eyes again and slowly read out what was written on the brass plaque:

"Henry Jekyll, MD, DCL, LLD, FRS."

"Henry *Jekyll*?" echoed Albert. "Did you say *Jekyll*? *Doctor* Jekyll? As in Doctor Jekyll and Mister—"

He broke off at the sound of rusty bolts being drawn on the other side of the worn, dark door.

"Somebody's coming, Dad," said Henry, swallowing hard. "Shall we do a runner?"

Albert nodded, wide-eyed, and turned, quickly – but his sudden movement caused another sharp pain to shoot up his back. "Oooh-er! I couldn't run if I tried, Henry," he groaned. "I don't think I could even *limp* in my present condition!"

"Yes, you can, Dad!" urged Henry. "Lean on me, we'll go together!"

But he spoke too late.

Before Albert had time to rest his elbow on his son's shoulder, the dark oak door creaked slowly open and an old man's voice addressed them from within.

31

"Good evening to you both," it said. "Don't be afraid – do come in."

Henry Hollins and his father looked doubtful but then, deciding that they had little choice, stepped through the open door and into the shadowy panelled entrance hall of Doctor Henry Jekyll's house.

3

As the front door closed behind them, Henry and Albert Hollins looked into the smiling face of the old man who had invited them inside. He had grey side-whiskers and was wearing rimless spectacles perched on the very end of his nose. His shabby, shapeless suit looked old fashioned and fitted him badly – almost as if it was something he had found crumpled up in a trunk in somebody else's attic.

He was a kindly-looking old gentleman, though, and Henry and Albert both smiled to themselves at their foolishness in having been afraid of entering the house.

There was one curious thing: the only light in the hall came from an oil lamp which the old gentleman was holding up above his head.

"Are you Doctor Jekyll?" asked Henry.

"I am!" said the old man, broadening his smile. "I am indeed!"

"Has there been a power cut?" asked Albert, nodding at the oil lamp.

But the doctor did not appear to have heard the question.

"Follow me, gentlemen," he said, leading the way along the dark-panelled hall.

It has to be said that Albert Hollins did have some *slight* misgivings as he looked around the surgery into which the doctor had shown them. The furniture was old fashioned for one thing; for another, the bottles and jars that stood along the shelves of a tall cabinet were covered in dust and cobwebs.

"Now *that* can't be very hygienic," Albert said to himself.

But it was too late now to walk out. In any case, his back was still giving him considerable pain. It seemed to Albert at that moment that any doctor was better than no doctor at all.

"Which one of you is the patient?" asked Doctor Jekyll, setting the oil lamp down on the top of his ancient roll-top desk.

"It's Dad," said Henry. "It's his back. He keeps getting these pains. Mum says that he's got garden gnome's disease."

"I haven't got anything of the kind," snorted Albert.

Albert Hollins always felt that garden gnome's

disease sounded rather silly. But the doctor did not appear to find the complaint at all amusing.

"I see, I see," he said, taking off his shabby old jacket and rolling up the frayed cuffs of his equally shabby old shirt. "Just slip your coat off, Mr . . . er . . . er . . .?"

"Hollins," said Henry. "My dad's called Albert Hollins."

"I'm afraid I don't know my National Health number," said Albert. "You see, we're only in London for the weekend and—"

"Oh, that's of no consequence to me, Mr Hollins," said the doctor. "That doesn't matter at all. Now, let's have that coat off, shall we?"

Albert Hollins, albeit reluctantly, allowed the old man to help him off with his jacket and the diamond-patterned pullover that Emily had knitted for his last birthday. Moments later, he found himself lying full length, stomach down, shirt rolled up, on an ancient horsehair sofa which was prickly to his bare skin.

Doctor Jekyll's hands went to work on the small of Albert's back. He seemed to find the source of the trouble right away.

"Ow-er!" went Albert.

"I am sorry," said the doctor. "I didn't mean to hurt you." His hands moved to another spot. "What happens if I press there?"

"Oooooh!"

"And how about there?"

"Ouch!"

"And just about there?"

"Aaaaaaaggghhhh!"

"Hmmm, hmmm," murmured the doctor, rolling down his sleeves again. "I see, I see."

"What is it, doctor? What have I done?" asked Albert, nervously.

"Nothing serious, Mr Hollins. Nothing to get alarmed about, I assure you. Nothing that a little medication won't put right. You can put your things back on again – we'll soon have you fit and well. And then you and your boy can get down to the serious business of enjoying your weekend in London. Isn't that right, lad?" said the old doctor, turning to Henry who was sitting on a hardbacked chair in a corner of the surgery.

"I'll say!" said Henry, enthusiastically.

"Ah, yes!" said Doctor Jekyll. "London is such a wonderful place for a boy of your years. So many exciting places to visit. So many wonderful, joyful things for a bright young lad to do! Visit the Chamber of Horrors, eh? Explore the terrors of the London Dungeon. Go sightseeing in the Bloody Tower. Stand on the very spot where Mary Queen of Scots had her head chopped off! Ah, what it is to be young, eh, Master Hollins? What's your first name, lad?"

"Henry, Doctor," said Henry, who had been nodding blissfully at every word.

"Another Henry!" said the doctor, beaming his broad smile again and rubbing his hands together. "The same as me! I was christened after my great-grandfather, you know. He was a Doctor Henry Jekyll, too."

"He wasn't *the* Doctor Jekyll, was he, Doctor?" asked Albert, who was sitting up again and pulling on his pullover. "Not the Doctor Jekyll that changed into . . ."

"The Doctor Jekyll that changed into an evil monster, is that what you were about to say?" snapped the old man.

"N-n-n-no," stuttered Albert.

"It doesn't matter." Doctor Jekyll's frown vanished as swiftly as it had arrived. "I have heard that story too many times before. How my great-grandfather invented a strange and terrible potion that turned him into the mad Mr Hyde." Doctor Jekyll paused, shook his head, and turned again to Henry. "They are all stories, Henry. All made-up stories. Nothing but stories. All lies."

"Isn't any of it true then?" asked Henry.

"Not a single word of it. But I have had to live with that legend all my life. Why else, do you imagine, am I practising in this forgotten backwater? Why else, do you imagine, is my waiting room empty and your father my only patient? I'll tell you why, Henry – because people, with their silly superstitions, refuse to bring their sicknesses and ailments to a doctor who bears the name of Henry Jekyll."

"Couldn't you change your name?" asked Henry.

"Why should I? My father was Doctor Jekyll; his father was Doctor Jekyll; his father's father was Doctor Jekyll. I am proud that I too am Doctor Jekyll. Why should I change it?"

"But if it isn't true about your great-grandfather changing into a ..." Henry's voice trailed away as he hesitated, wondering whether the word he was about to use might hurt the doctor's feelings regarding his ancestor.

But he need not have worried.

"Into an evil monster?" said Doctor Jekyll, finishing Henry's sentence for him.

"Mmmm," murmured Henry, nodding his head. "If it *isn't* true – how did the story start?"

"How does any malicious tale begin?" replied the doctor, shrugging as he spread his hands apart, palms upward. "By gossip, my boy. By intrigue, born of jealousy. Because someone, somewhere, on some particular rainy day had nothing better to do, so he invented an impossible story. Who knows?" The doctor sat down in the old fashioned carved wood chair that stood in front of his roll-top desk. "I will show you something," he said. "Something I have kept tucked away safely down all the years – something my father handed on to me that had been handed on to him by *his* father."

The doctor unlocked the bottom drawer of his desk, rifled through the stack of files and documents inside, and took out a small envelope that had been hidden away at the very bottom. He opened the envelope, took out the single piece of paper that was inside, and proffered it to Henry.

"What do you think of that?" asked Doctor Jekyll.

Henry took the sheet of paper and unfolded it carefully. It was as yellow with age as the envelope that had contained it. "It's just a piece of paper," he said, passing it to his father.

"With writing on it," said Mr Hollins. "In a foreign language. Come on, Henry, you're the scholar in the family. Now's the time to start polishing up that French they've been teaching you in school."

"It's not in French, Dad," said Henry.

"All right then – German."

"It's not in German either," said Henry who, although he was not much good at *reading* foreign languages, at least could *recognize* them. "Is it Latin?" he said, turning to Doctor Jekyll.

"Quite so," said the doctor.

"I don't do Latin," said Henry.

"What you see written down there is supposed to be the formula invented by my father's father's father – the secret potion, it is said, that turned him from the law-abiding Doctor Henry Jekyll into the foul monster, Edward Hyde."

"Golly!" said Henry.

"Well I never!" said Albert, shivering slightly as he quickly handed the piece of paper back to Henry. "Put it down on the desk, son. You want to keep that somewhere safe, doctor."

"Thank you," said Doctor Jekyll, as Henry placed the formula in front of him. "It *is* safe with me," the doctor continued, turning back to Mr Hollins. "It will go back inside the very same drawer where it has lain untouched for all these years."

"Shouldn't you keep it in a safe?" suggested Henry.

"Or better still, burn it?" vouchsafed his father.

"Why should I do that?" asked Doctor Jekyll.

"I would, if it were mine," said Mr Hollins, with a gulp.

The doctor smiled at Albert. "Destroy a harmless piece of paper? he said. "It is of neither use nor value except for idle amusement. I've already told you, there is not a word of truth in the legend regarding my great-grandfather."

"But if there *is* a formula, isn't that proof that—"

"It is no more than a playful prank, I assure you, Mr Hollins," interrupted the doctor. "My father's grandfather wrote it out, I'm sure, only to fool those that tried to shame his name. But it has been kept in the family all these years in memory of that same very first Doctor Henry Jekyll." While he was speaking, the doctor had been writing out a prescription for some medication for Albert's aching back. As he finished this task, he got to his feet, picked up his shabby crumpled jacket and slipped it on. He pulled at a gold chain that hung across his waistcoat and lifted a large old-fashioned watch out of his pocket. "Good heavens, is that the time!" he said, peering at the watch face. "If you are ready, Mr Hollins, I shall bid you both goodnight and lock up the surgery."

"It isn't quite eight o'clock yet, doctor," said Albert, looking at his watch. "You never know, there's still time for more customers to turn up."

Doctor Jekyll smiled again – but this smile was sadder than the ones before. "No – no," he said, with a shake of his head. "They will not come here. You were the first patient to walk through my door since . . . who knows when? The fools – they will not come to consult Doctor Henry Jekyll."

"I don't know why not, doctor," said Albert, stoutly. "I don't know what you did to my back when you pushed and pummelled it about, but it's starting to feel better already. I shall certainly recommend your name when I get back to the hotel – I shall recommend it very highly indeed."

"You are most kind," replied the doctor, with a sigh, "but it makes no matter, I am getting old . . . perhaps it is time for me to retire . . . who knows, perhaps I have just attended to the needs of my very last patient . . ." As he spoke, Doctor Jekyll picked up the flickering oil lamp and moved towards the surgery door. He opened the door and glanced down the hall, which was lined with wooden chairs. "What did I say?" he said, with another sad sigh. "Not a single person waiting to see me."

Albert and Henry Hollins exchanged a glance and then smiled at Doctor Jekyll, sympathetically. But there was nothing they could say that might cheer him up. The corridor *was* empty. There *were* no patients waiting to consult the doctor. They moved to follow him down the hall.

"Just a moment!" exclaimed the doctor, looking back into the surgery. "You are forgetting your prescription, Mr Hollins."

"Trust me!" joked Albert, going back and picking up the slip of paper from the doctor's desk. "Emily keeps telling me that I'd forget my head if it wasn't fastened on!" Then, folding the prescription in half, he tucked it into his inside pocket for safe-keeping and followed Henry and the doctor along the hall.

"Goodnight to you," said Doctor Jekyll, holding the lamp shoulder high as he opened the front door. "Goodnight to you both!"

"Goodnight, Doctor," said Albert, stepping out into the empty moonlit cobbled square.

"Goodnight, Doctor Jekyll," said Henry, following his father.

The heavy oak door creaked shut behind them.

"Whoo-ooo!" went the owl, softly this time, high up in the branches of its tree.

Albert Hollins shivered and pulled his jacket collar up around his ears. He felt a sudden chill, even though the evening was quite warm. "What a queer old chap," he murmured.

"I thought he was great, Dad," said Henry, his voice full of enthusiasm. "A real life Doctor Henry Jekyll! Wait till I tell the kids at school!"

"Yes, well . . ." replied his father, none too surely, "it's a good job I'm a level-headed sort of chap who doesn't go in for all this horror story stuff and nonsense—" He broke off as the owl hooted once again. "Come along, Henry," he said briskly. "Let's get a move on – your mother must be wondering where we've got to."

They quickened their pace and the cobbled moonlit square echoed to the sound of their scurrying footsteps. A moment later they had disappeared into the shadows of the dark narrow passage and the square was silent once more.

Next morning, in the brightly lit, busy breakfast room of the Hotel Emilion, with its colourful gloss-painted furniture and with Muzak playing in the background, it seemed to Henry Hollins as if the quaint square with its curious flickering gas lamp had almost been a dream.

Henry was sitting with his mother and father at a corner table, right next to a giant shiny-leafed rubber plant in a big red plastic pot. The three Hollinses were studying plastic-coated breakfast menus.

"Good morning, Diamond-Days weekenders!" said a cheery voice.

Albert, Emily and Henry peered over the tops of their menus at the figure hovering by their table, notepad and ballpoint pen at the ready.

"Why, it's Mr Perkins, the hotel porter, isn't it?" said Emily, instantly recognizing the man who had kindly assisted them upstairs with their luggage the previous afternoon.

"Perkins, yes, Mrs Hollins – porter, no – not at this immediate moment," said Mr Perkins. "I've got my waiter's hat on this morning, figuratively speaking. Waiter's white jacket, I suppose I should say – waiters don't wear hats, do they? We're a bit short-staffed waiter-wise, so I'm giving them a hand." He scratched his ear with the tip of his ballpoint pen, then grinned at Henry and winked. "Good morning, youngest Hollins!" he said.

"Good morning, Mr Perkins," replied Henry, smiling back at him.

"And how's the back this morning, Mr Hollins?" continued Perkins, turning to Albert.

"Very tender, Mr Perkins," replied Albert, with a sigh. "I didn't do myself any good at all last night, lifting up that heavy suitcase."

"You managed to find that doctor's surgery though, I hope?"

"Indeed we did, thanks to your directions," said Albert. "And very useful he proved to be too."

"His name's Doctor Henry Jekyll, Mr Perkins," announced Henry.

"Well, I never!" said Perkins, raising his eyebrows in surprise.

"I don't care if his name's Doctor Frankenstein," said Emily, sternly. "It's no good going to see a doctor, Albert, if you don't take his advice. You want to find a chemist's shop this morning and get that prescription made up that he wrote out for you – it won't cure anything while it's sitting in your wallet."

"I intend to get it made up, Emily," replied Albert. "As a matter of fact, I've got a chemist's shop at the very top of my priorities this morning – as soon as I've had some breakfast."

"Exactly what I'm here for!" said Perkins, giving Henry another broad wink then, turning back to Albert, he added, "For starters, Mr Hollins, might I recommend the orange juice?"

"Is it fresh?" asked Albert.

"I opened the carton myself only this morning."

"Wheel it in!" said Mr Hollins.

"Three orange juices," said Perkins, jotting down the order on his notepad and then, as he continued, he ticked off on his fingers the delights to come, "followed by the crunchy cornflakes; the rasher of streaky bacon; the succulent plump pork sausage; the tasty English mushroom; the grilled Jersey tomato and the crisp fried slice of bread surmounted by the runny fried egg."

"That sounds great!" said Henry.

"Are we entitled to all that?" gasped Albert.

"You are indeed, Mr Hollins. *And* fresh baked breakfast rolls plus your individual choice of tea or coffee – as privileged Diamond-Days weekenders you're entitled to go right through the card."

"Tea for three then, please," said Emily. "But don't bring me the full English fry-up – I'll just have the orange juice, the cornflakes and perhaps a slice of toast."

Perkins looked disappointed. "Are you *quite* sure

that I can't tempt you to the full treatment?" he asked, anxiously. "There's nothing extra to pay, you know – it's all inclusive."

"Oh, go on then – you've talked me into it," said Emily, settling herself on her chair in readiness for the feast to come.

"Good!" said the delighted Perkins. "I'll have your orange juice here in two shakes of a lamb's tail!" He added a final squiggle to his notepad and set off in the direction of the kitchens.

Emily glanced inquisitively round the busy breakfast room. "Hey!" she cried, nudging Albert in the ribs. "Look who's just walked through the door! It's that nice hostess who was on our coach . . . What's she call herself?"

"Debbie," whispered Henry, as the smart young lady threaded her way through the busy tables towards the corner where they were sitting.

"Well! What a coincidence!" said the in-coach hostess, favouring the Hollinses with a cheery smile. "What a small world! Good morning, Mr and Mrs Hollins – good morning, Henry!"

"Good morning, Debbie!" they chorused in reply.

"You *are* up bright and early this morning," said the hostess.

"Well, you have to be, don't you?" replied Emily, fiddling with the strap on her handbag. "You need to make an early start if you've all your sightseeing to do in a day and a half."

"Good morning, Deborah!" cried Perkins, returning with a tray on which he was carrying three glasses of orange juice.

"Hello, Reggie!"

"You two seem to know each other," observed Emily.

"We do indeed," chuckled Perkins.

"We ought to," grinned Debbie.

"Deborah's one of our most highly esteemed regular customers," Perkins told the Hollinses. "She's one of your real-life jetsetters is our Miss Debs. Why – she's up and down that M1 motorway like nobody's business."

He set down the glasses of orange juice in front of Albert, Henry and Emily and, turning to Debbie, went on: "I've got your usual table saved for you, Deborah – if you'd care to take a seat, I'll have your muesli, coffee and hot croissant in two shakes of a gnat's bottom."

"Thanks, Reggie," said Deborah, giving the porter one of her warmest smiles.

"And three helpings of cornflakes, bacon and egg and all the trimmings coming up," and, so saying, Perkins turned and strode off towards the kitchens, humming a merry little tune to himself and drumming his fingers on the empty tray.

"What's on the itinerary this morning then?" Debbie asked the Hollinses.

Albert scratched his head and shrugged. "We haven't even thought about it yet," he said.

"I have!" said Henry. "What about the Chamber of Horrors first and then a trip to the London Dungeon?"

Emily shivered and pulled a face. "I'm not sure that *I'll* be up to anything quite so blood-curdling," she said. "Not straight after a big fry-up breakfast, anyway."

"She's right, Henry," agreed Albert. "We'll do those places this afternoon – this morning we'll do the sort of open-air things – like Hyde Park, for instance."

"Carnaby Street?" asked Henry.

"Why not?" said his father. "And Westminster Abbey."

"You know what you can't afford to miss out, don't you?" said Debbie.

Albert, Emily and Henry gazed at her with keen interest and shook their heads. They didn't know what it was that they couldn't afford to miss out.

"Buckingham Palace, of course!" said Debbie.

Emily nodded firmly. "There you are, you see!" she said to her husband and her son. "That's somewhere you'd forgotten to put on your list!"

"True," said Albert.

"You'll kill two birds with one stone as well," Debbie told them. "They're Trooping the Colour this morning on Horse Guards Parade – you'll see them coming back down the Mall on their way to the barracks."

"Ace!" said Henry.

"We'll have a basinful of that!" said Albert.

But Emily was not so sure. "I don't know that I fancy getting pushed and pulled around in all them crowds," she said. "Why don't you two take yourselves off there, while I take a quiet stroll around the department stores in Oxford Street and Regent Street? And then, afterwards, we could all meet up here again for lunch."

"Sounds like a good idea to me," said Albert.

"If you're looking round the shops, Mrs Hollins, you want to take yourself off to Marks & Spencer at Marble Arch," advised Debbie.

"Oh, we've got a Marks & Sparks at home in Staplewood," said Emily.

"Ah – but the stuff you get at *your* Marks & Sparks isn't the same sort of stuff at all as you get at Marks & Sparks in London."

"Isn't it?" asked Emily, in some surprise.

"Not a bit," said the well-informed hostess.

"And if Debbie says it isn't, you can bet your cotton socks it's not," said Perkins, arriving on the scene again – this time with three bowls of cornflakes on his tray.

"Well!" said Albert, raising his eyebrows. "You live and learn!"

"She knows her way round, does Debbie," Perkins continued, proudly. "I've told you – she's a regular jetsetter." He put the bowls of cornflakes down in front of the Hollins family and then nodded across at an empty table set for one. "Your muesli's ready and waiting for you, Debbie – and don't let your coffee go cold neither."

"Thanks, Reggie," said Debbie, favouring the porter-turned-waiter with one of her widest smiles then, turning towards the Hollinses, she added, "Have a nice day, you lot!"

"And you!" said Emily.

"Toodle-pip!" said Albert.

"Bye!" said Henry.

"Enjoy your cornflakes," Perkins said to the Hollinses. "And just you wait until you see the spread our breakfast chef's cooking up for you – enough to feed a regiment! He's even slipped you a slice of fried black pudding each! *Bon appetit!*"

"*Merci beaucoup!*" said Albert, not to be outdone. "So that's the schedule then, is it?" he continued, after Perkins had gone. "It's you and me for the palace, Henry, while your mum goes window-shopping. Hey – and speaking of shops reminds me – the very first thing we've got to do is pop into a chemist's shop and get this prescription made up."

As he spoke, Albert Hollins patted the left side of his chest where in his inside pocket lay the folded slip of paper he had picked up from Doctor Henry Jekyll's ancient roll-top desk.

4

The chemist's that Henry and Albert found was more like a department store than a shop and was much busier, too, than the one they used back home in Stapleford. It took them some time to find the counter where the prescriptions were dispensed but, once they *did* find it, they were pleased to discover only two or three other customers waiting for their medicines to be made up.

"Don't go too far away, Henry," warned Albert as his son drifted off towards the computer counter. "I shouldn't think this is going to take very long."

"I won't, Dad – I'll just be over here," said Henry, examining the display of computer tapes.

But Albert Hollins was wrong.

He was kept waiting for some time – almost three-quarters of an hour, in fact. What was more, he noticed, not only had everyone in front of him been served and gone, but other people had arrived, handed over their prescriptions, waited, then left clutching their packages containing bottles, jars and ointments.

Albert Hollins shuffled impatiently on his hard chair. "Come on, come on!" he muttered under his breath. "We'll be here all day at this rate – a fine weekend's holiday this is turning out to be – stuck sitting in a chemist's shop!"

Finally he was put out of his misery.

"Hollins?" called a young lady, wearing a spotless white smock, as she scurried out through the door behind which the prescriptions were dispensed. "Is there a Mr Albert Hollins waiting?"

"Here!" called Albert, jumping to his feet. "Come on, Henry – it's us at long last!" he called across to his son as he moved up to the counter.

Henry Hollins dragged himself away from the bank upon bank of computer tapes, many of which were new to him, and went to stand at his father's side.

Albert was ready to give the young lady a piece of his mind. He had, in fact, been practising what he would say: "If we kept our customers waiting as long as this, young woman, the bottom would drop right out of the garden-gnome market!" But the young lady gave him such an apologetic smile that his anger evaporated instantly.

"I'm sorry you've been kept waiting for such a long time, Mr Hollins," she said, putting a bottle into a paper bag.

"That's quite all right," mumbled Albert.

"You see, there were one or two ingredients in your prescription that we don't normally stock."

"Oh, really?" said Albert.

"Mmmmm," said the young lady with a nod. "We don't have much call for them these days – there was the lizard liver for a start."

"Lizard liver?" gulped Albert.

"Yuk!" went Henry.

"And then there was the powdered bat's wing – we don't normally keep either of those on the National Health. And that's saying nothing of the Tincture of Toad's Tongue."

"I see," said Albert, weakly.

"We've had to send a messenger on a motorbike to fetch them from our head office right across London."

"Oh dear me!" said Albert. "I do hope I haven't put you to too much trouble?"

"Not at all, Mr Hollins," said the young lady pleasantly. "It's what we're here for. That'll be two pounds forty, sir. The directions are written on the label."

"Thanks very much, miss," said Albert, handing her the money and taking the package in return.

"Have a nice day now, both of you!" she called out to them as they moved away from the counter.

In next to no time at all, they were on the bus

that Perkins had told them would best get them to their destination.

"Welcome aboard the forty-three, mister – you too, young man!" said the affable West Indian conductor as the bus pulled away from the bus stop. "And where exactly might the pair of you be heading?"

"One and a half to Buckingham Palace, please," said Albert, proffering a handful of coins.

"One and a half to Victoria Station, you mean," replied the conductor, handing the tickets to Henry and taking the correct amount of money out of Albert's palm. "We don't go all the way to the palace," he explained, "but you won't have very far to walk."

"Can we go upstairs, Dad?" asked Henry.

"I don't see why not," replied Albert.

"You'll have it all to yourselves up there," said the conductor. "I don't know where all the passengers have gone this morning – it's like cruising round London on a dieselized *Marie Celeste*!"

"I bet they're all at the Horse Guards Parade," Henry told him. "They're Trooping the Colour this morning – we're going to watch them march back along the Mall."

"Is that a fact, young man?" said the conductor, grinning at Albert.

"Up you go, Henry," said Albert Hollins, indicating the flight of stairs.

"Can we sit at the front, Dad?" asked Henry.

"Wherever you like," said Albert, following his son along the empty deck towards the seats at the very front. "I'll tell you what you can do for me," he continued, sitting down beside Henry and pulling the package he had got at the chemist's out of his pocket. "You can read out the instructions on this bottle – I've left my glasses back at the hotel. Does it say how often I'm supposed to rub it on?"

Henry took the bottle from his father and studied the label on the front. "'The mixture – Two Tablespoonfuls To Be Taken After Meals . . .' You're not supposed to rub it on, Dad, you're supposed to swallow it."

"*Swallow* it?" said Albert, pulling a face. "Are you *sure* that's what it says? I thought he'd given me some sort of embrocation."

"Two tablespoonfuls to be *taken*, Dad – that's what's written on here."

"I'm not too sure I fancy that, Henry," said Albert, with a frown. "Do you remember the things that young lady in the chemist's shop said this stuff had got inside it? Powdered bat's wing! Lizard's liver!"

"Tincture of Toad's Tongue," said Henry.

"Don't remind me, lad!" said Albert, pulling

another face. He took the bottle back from Henry, unscrewed the cap and sniffed at the contents. "*Pooh*!" he said.

"What does it smell like, Dad?"

"Not too good," said Albert, holding the bottle up to the light and peering at its unappetizing grey-greeny contents. "Oh, well," he said, with a shrug. "Let's hope that Doctor Jekyll knew what he was doing! I'll try a swig."

"Have you got a tablespoon, Dad?"

"It's a curious fact of life, Henry, but tablespoons – indeed, most forms of domestic cutlery – are rather less than readily available on the top deck of a London bus."

"How will you know how much to take then?"

"I'll hazard a guess. Cheers!" And, so saying, he put the bottle to his lips and took a long pull at the medicine. Albert's Adam's apple went up and down and then he spluttered, coughed, blinked hard and shook his head. "*Uuugghhh*!"

"What's it like, Dad?" asked Henry, anxious for his father's well-being.

"*Coorrr!*" said Albert, lost for immediate words. He smacked his lips and ran his tongue round the inside of his mouth, trying to rid himself of the awful aftertaste.

"What does it taste of?" asked Henry.

"Rather akin, I'd say, to lizard's liver," said

Albert, reflectively. "If I knew what lizard's liver tasted like – with the added distinctive flavour of powdered bat's wing. Not forgetting, of course, the piquant tang of Tincture of Toad's Tongue – and several other things I'd rather not go into, thank you very much . . . In a nutshell, Henry, it tastes *rotten*!"

There was a long silence during which Albert Hollins sat hunched in his seat and gazed out of the window pensively. They were cruising down Park Lane and passing some of London's grand, imposing, famous hotels: Grosvenor House; The Dorchester; The London Hilton. On the other side of the bus, the green grass and tall trees of Hyde Park stretched away before their eyes. Ahead of them lay Hyde Park Corner. But Albert Hollins was not taking in any of this. He smacked his lips and groaned again.

"I've got some mints in my pocket, Dad, if you want something to take the taste away," Henry ventured at last. "Except that they're not very clean."

"No, thanks, Henry," replied Albert, managing a rueful smile as he slipped the bottle of medicine back into his jacket pocket. "Roll on Buckingham Palace, eh? And let's hope that the worst part of the day is over!"

They were brave words which Henry's father

would have cause to consider before the afternoon was out – for the worst part of Albert Hollins's day was by no means over. The worst by far, in fact, was yet to come . . .

"Can you see anything, Dad?" asked Henry, excitedly, standing on tiptoe and trying to peer over the shoulder of the American lady with the headscarf covered with a map of the USA who was standing in front of him.

"Not any more than you, Henry," replied Albert, whose vision was completely blocked by the two tall camera-bedecked foreign tourists who were chattering to each other in their own language. "Trust me to get stuck behind the only pair of giant-sized Japanese in London," he grumbled.

Henry and his father had arrived outside Buckingham Palace just in time for the march past of the Guards Regiment on their way back from the Trooping of the Colour. Already, they could hear the sound of the military band moving towards them down the Mall. But although they could *hear* what was going on, they were unable to *see* anything at all. Other visitors and tourists had got there before them in their thousands. Albert Hollins and his son found themselves standing up against the Palace railings at the very back of the crowded pavement.

"If we hadn't spent half the morning waiting in that chemist's shop," grumbled Albert, "we'd have been at the front of these lot – not behind them!"

"The band sounds brill though," said Henry. "Even if we don't see them march past, at least we'll be able to listen to the music."

"Speaking of chemist's shops, Henry," said Albert, looking puzzled, "I . . . I don't think that medicine did me any good – in fact, I'm beginning to feel rather—"

He broke off, suddenly. "Ooooh-er!" he cried, rather sharply.

"Is it your back again, Dad?" asked Henry. "Did you have another twinge?"

Mr Hollins shook his head. "It wasn't my back, son, no. I . . . I don't rightly know what it was. I just felt a sort of funny sensation all over me . . . *Ohhh*! There it goes again!" he said and, as he spoke, he shivered violently.

"Are you feeling all right, Dad?" asked Henry, in some concern. "Shall we see if we can get a cab and go back to the hotel?"

"No, no, no – we'd never get one in all this c-c-c-crush," stammered Albert, who was now twitching visibly from head to foot.

"But you ought to see a doctor, Dad, if you're not well."

"I . . . I d-d-d-don't feel ill, Henry – I just f-f-f-feel . . . well . . . *unusual*."

"How do you mean, 'unusual'?" asked Henry.

"R-r-r-r-rather odd," stuttered Albert, as another of the spasms took hold of him. "As a matter of f-f-f-fact, it's not entirely an unpleasant sensation at all – it's a k-k-k-kind of all-over t-t-t-tickling feeling."

As well as having a stutter, Albert's voice seemed to have deepened and become harsher.

Henry stared into his father's face – and what he saw there worried him still further. "Hey, Dad!" he said, in puzzled tones. "Did you have a shave this morning?"

"Of c-c-c-course I did!" replied Albert, almost in a growl.

"But your face – it's . . . it's going all hairy, Dad! All hairy and sort of wrinkled!"

"Don't talk daft, lad!" replied Albert, hoarsely.

But, putting his hands up to his cheeks, he discovered that what Henry had told him was true. The face that he had shaved so carefully in the gleaming bathroom at the Hotel Emilion only a couple of hours before – the same face that had smiled back at him all smooth and tidy in the bathroom mirror – was now covered in bristly *hair*! Also, again as Henry had said, it felt sort of . . . well . . . wrinkled and all leathery too!

"What . . . What's happened to me?" he murmured nervously, in the new low voice that now came out of his throat.

Then, as he took his trembling hands away from his face, he was horrified to see that the backs of them were also covered in thick, black hair.

Albert Hollins hung his head and let out a long, sad sigh of despair – at least, he had *meant* to let out a long, sad sigh of despair but what came out of his mouth sounded more like the anguished howl of some four-footed beast of the forest.

Luckily for Albert, while his strange transformation had been taking place, the parade had moved on and the Guards band was now swinging past Buckingham Palace – the stirring sound of the pipes and drums, accompanied by the cheers of the crowds, had drowned his animal cry.

It was lucky too, Henry told himself, that he and his father were standing at the very back of the throng – for it meant none of the spectators had noticed that, up against the palace railings, one of their number was slowly turning into a horrible hairy monster.

But this was of little consolation to Albert. "What's happened to me, Henry?" he croaked. "What am I going to *do*?"

Henry thought hard and fast.

"Pull your coat collar up around your ears, Dad, and tuck your face down too," he said.

Albert did as his son suggested, and, a moment later, only the top of his head was visible over his upturned collar.

"But I can't go around like this, Henry!" moaned Albert, gruffly. "What will people think? Besides – I can't see where I'm going."

"I'll lead you, Dad," said Henry, taking his father by the hand. "There's a park across the road – if we can run over there while everybody's still watching the soldiers march past, we might find somewhere for you to hide." He tugged at his father's hand, but Albert held fast and refused to budge.

"I can't spend the rest of my days holed up in

St James's Park!" Albert objected, hoarsely, his voice coming from somewhere down inside his coat.

"Only until we *think* of something, Dad," Henry pleaded. "Come *on*! If we don't go now, the parade will all be over and then *everybody's* going to see you!"

Albert needed no further urging. Head tucked down inside his jacket and unable to see a thing, he kept a tight hold on Henry's hand as they set off, running as fast as they were able around the back of the cheering throng.

They reached the safety of the park unnoticed. It was empty, as Henry had guessed it would be. All the visitors and foreign tourists were gathered on the pavements along the Mall and outside the palace, watching the splendid parade march past. But, just to be on the safe side, Henry led his father further away from the noise along a deserted path that took them down to a tree-lined lake. The only sound was the constant quacking of ducks.

"You can come out now, Dad, if you like," suggested Henry.

Albert's head rose up, tortoise-like, from his upturned collar. His hairy, wrinkled face peered nervously around. Then, after satisfying himself that there wasn't anyone about, he sat down heavily on a green park bench on the path beside the lake. Now that the danger of immediate discovery was over, there was time for him to consider his terrible plight.

"What . . . what's happened to me, Henry?" he croaked. "And what's happened to my voice?" He felt at his face and then examined the backs of his hands again. "I must look *awful*!"

Henry Hollins shrugged. His father *did* look awful. Not to mince words, in fact, he looked like a horrible hairy monster. But, monster or no monster, the figure sitting slumped on the park bench was still his dad. It was up to Henry to keep his father's spirits up.

"You don't look *too* bad, Dad," said Henry. "I've seen worse."

"Yes, in a late night horror film on the telly, I suppose?" moaned Albert, dejectedly.

A grey-green duck with an orange beak scrambled out of the lake, shook its wings, looked up into Albert's face, then turned and instantly waddled off again.

"Did you see that?" Albert whimpered. "Even the flippin' ducks can't stand the sight of me!"

"I don't think it's that at all, Dad," said Henry, loyally. "I think it's because you haven't brought any bits of bread."

But Albert was not to be consoled. "Good grief!" he wailed. "What's to become of me! I'm a laughing stock! My face doesn't feel as if it's mine any more – it feels as if it belongs to King Kong! It's all that chemist's fault!"

Henry shook his head. He had been turning over in his mind the sequence of events. He was convinced where the blame lay.

"I don't think it was the chemist's fault, Dad."

"It *was*, Henry," Albert insisted, quite sure in his own mind. "Just wait till I get my hairy hands on him! I'll . . . I'll . . ."

"Don't get upset, Dad!" Henry broke in, nervously.

Albert Hollins's strange low voice had suddenly begun to sound disturbingly menacing and Henry was worried that, as well as *looking* like a monster, his father was about to become one! Henry need not have worried – his father's flash of temper vanished as quickly as it had come. He was his same sad self again.

"I know just what that chemist's done," he murmured, choking back a sob. "He's given me the wrong prescription." He stared down at his hairy hands. "I'll bet he's given me another customer's hair restorer. It needed rubbing on to somebody's bald head, did that stuff – it was never intended to be swallowed . . ." Albert paused and his eyes widened in horror as what he thought to be the truth struck home. "And *I* swallowed it!" he gulped.

67

"Good heavens, Henry, I swallowed *hair restorer*! If it's done this to my hands and face – what the hummers has it done to my *insides*? My stomach must be all hairy too! Hairy stomach, hairy liver, hairy lungs . . . I've probably got a hairy heart! I'll spifflicate that chemist, Henry! I'll take him to court for every penny he possesses . . ." Albert paused again. His shoulders drooped. He shook his head and continued, sadly, "What am I talking about? I *can't* take him to court. I can't take anyone to court in this condition. What chance would I stand in the witness box looking like this?"

"It *wasn't* the chemist's fault, Dad – *truly*," said Henry, choosing his words carefully, not wishing to alarm his father further. "And I'm sorry to have to tell you that there's more bad news."

Albert Hollins peered at his son from underneath a pair of new-grown black bushy eyebrows. *More* bad news? What possible horrors could be piled upon his present horrible condition?

"Go on," growled Albert.

"The chemist made you up the *right* prescription, Dad – I mean, he made up the prescription that you gave him – but the prescription that you gave him was the *wrong* prescription."

"The right prescription was the wrong prescription?" Albert Hollins frowned and his bushy eyebrows met above his nose, "Talk sense, Henry!"

he snapped. "I've enough on my plate without you contradicting yourself."

"It was *you* that gave him the *wrong* prescription – don't you remember? You must have picked up the other one by mistake from Doctor Jekyll's desk."

"Other one? What other one?" Albert Hollins's wrinkled face was suddenly pale. "Not the one that . . .?"

Henry nodded glumly. "The one that belonged to his great-grandfather," he said.

"Fizzin' heckers!" groaned Albert. "Henry, you've hit the nail spot on the head! Oh, my sainted stars! You know what this means, don't you?"

"Yes, Dad."

"It means that I'm not *me* any longer! I'm not Albert Hollins – I've turned into Mr Edward Hyde!"

"Yes, Dad."

"Whatever will your mother say, when she finds out?" he whimpered. "And, what's even worse, what will the lads say on Monday morning when I turn up at the gates of the garden gnome factory – with all this flippin' hair all over my face? They'll probably think I've turned into a garden gnome!" With which, Albert buried his hairy face in his hairy hands.

"It might not be all that bad, Dad," said Henry.

"Not that bad? Not that bad!" stormed Albert. "Good grief, son – *look* at me! It couldn't be any worse than this if it tried!"

"I mean, it might not last, Dad. You might not stay like that."

Albert Hollins slowly took his hands away from his face and gazed at his son. "Do you mean there's hope?" he asked, blinking back a tear.

Henry nodded again. "The real Mr Hyde didn't stay Mr Hyde for ever."

"Didn't he, Henry?"

This time Henry shook his head. "He turned back into Doctor Jekyll," he said.

"Can you swear to that?" asked Albert, who had not read the book about the famous doctor and his evil counterpart.

Albert Hollins, it should be said, was not a great one for reading. In fact, he rarely glanced at any printed matter apart from his daily newspaper and *Garden Gnomes Illustrated*, his regular monthly periodical.

"I'm absolutely positive, Dad," said Henry. To be truthful, Henry hadn't read the book himself, but he had seen the film on the telly. "He kept changing from one to the other. I think he changed from Doctor Jekyll into Mr Hyde and from Mr Hyde back to Doctor Jekyll quite a number of times."

"Oh, great!" grumbled Albert. "That's fantastic news. Thanks very much, son. Can you see me on a Saturday morning in the shopping precinct with your mother? She leaves me as per usual, looking into the window of the hi-fi shop while she pops into Marks & Sparks for a sliced wholemeal loaf. When she comes out, I'm not Albert Hollins any longer – I've changed into Edward Hyde for the umpteenth time and I'm running rampant, all hairy and horrible, right through Woollies and British Home Stores."

"But you won't be like the *real* Mr Hyde, Dad – he kept on drinking the mixture," Henry pointed out to his father. "Perhaps, if you don't take another dose, you'll go back to normal and *stay* normal."

"Me?" cried Albert, hoarsely. "Drink any more of that rotten muck? Is it likely? I wish I'd never set eyes on the foul stuff!" As he spoke, Albert Hollins tugged the bottle of medicine out of his pocket. "I'll show you how much more of this I'm going to drink, Henry—"

For one awful moment, Henry thought that his father was about to swallow another mouthful of the strange concoction, but he was reassured to see Albert draw back his arm and throw the bottle as far as he was able. It landed in the lake with a loud *plop*, disturbing an entire family of swimming ducks.

71

"That's where that evil jollop rightly belongs, Henry," growled Albert, wiping his hairy hands together in satisfaction. "And good riddance to bad rubbish!"

But Henry wasn't paying attention to his father. His face was turned towards the entrance to the park and his head was cocked on one side.

"Listen, Dad!"

"I can't hear anything," replied Albert, after having strained his ears for several seconds.

"That's what I mean," said Henry. "Neither can I. The parade must be over. The crowds will be coming into the park any minute. We can't stay here."

Albert Hollins got up from his park bench and walked nervously up and down the gravel path, slapping his arms against his sides. "We can't very well go anywhere else," he said. "We certainly can't get back to the hotel – can you see a bus conductor in his right mind letting me loose on his top deck looking like this? I'd frighten the life out of the other passengers."

Henry was forced to admit to himself that what his father had just said was true. Besides, to move back to the entrance of the park would only take them straight towards the thronging visitors and tourists they had not long run away from. It seemed that they were trapped. Henry Hollins glanced all around in desperation – and spotted something that might provide the answer to their seemingly impossible situation.

"There's a little island over there, Dad!" he cried, pointing out into the middle of the lake. "You could hide there in the bushes. I shouldn't think anything ever goes on it except ducks. Why don't you wade out now and keep out of sight, while I go back to the hotel for help?"

But Albert Hollins shook his head, firmly. "No, Henry," he croaked. "For the time being, if it's all the same to you, I'd rather that your mother was left in ignorance regarding my unfortunate condition."

"She's going to find out sooner or later, Dad."

"Perhaps she is, son – but later rather than sooner, if you don't mind. In any case, perhaps you were right – if God is good, I might very well go back to being normal. In which circumstance, Henry, the less your mother knows about what happened, the better. She'd never let me hear the end of it."

"Whatever you say, Dad," agreed Henry. "I wasn't thinking of Mum anyway – I was thinking of going to Mr Perkins."

Albert's leathery face looked even more wrinkled as he screwed it up in puzzled thought. "Who's Mr Perkins when he's at home?" he asked.

"You know Mr Perkins, Dad – the porter that we met when we arrived. He carried our suitcases up to the room for us. And he served us with our breakfasts this morning."

"Of course he did!" said Albert, snapping his fingers. "I'm sorry, Henry. I just can't seem to think straight – I suppose it's not surprising after all that's happened. But do you honestly think that Mr Perkins would want to get mixed up in this how-d'yer-do? It hardly falls inside the realm of his hotel porter's duties. And even if he *did* agree to help – what could he *do*?" Albert Hollins scuffed the toe of one shoe in the gravel on the path and added, sadly, "What could *anybody* do for that matter? It's *hopeless*!"

Henry shrugged and thought hard. "If he's got a car, he could drive it here and take you back to the hotel for a start, Dad," he suggested.

Albert Hollins was forced to admit that this, at least, was a possibility. "That's true," he conceded, nodding.

"Only if you *are* going to hide out on that island, Dad, you'd better get going," Henry insisted. Looking along the path and through the trees, he could see people beginning to drift into the park.

Albert sat down again on the bench and took off his shoes and socks. He rolled up his trouser legs and was further saddened to see that his legs had also sprouted a covering of coarse, black hair. But there was no time to ponder on that problem now. Albert knotted his shoelaces together, hung the shoes round his neck, tucked his socks inside his jacket pocket, stood up and dipped the end of his left big toe in the lake.

"Chuffing hummers, Henry!" he gasped. "It's freezing cold!"

"Hurry up, Dad!" urged Henry.

Time was running out for Albert Hollins.

"I'm on my way, son," he said, and then held his breath as he lowered both of his feet into the murky waters of the lake. "Oooooh, it is *chilly*!" he said with a shiver, as his feet sank into the mud and the water came up around his calves. Albert glanced up at Henry who was standing on the path above him. "If I'd known I was going paddling," he said, "I'd have booked us in at Blackpool!" With which, he set off bravely, wading out towards the little island and pausing only to call back, "I thought you said it wasn't deep, Henry! It's up to my knees already – my trouser-ends are sopping wet!"

Henry Hollins waited until his father had pulled himself up on to the island and was safely hidden from sight. Not until then did Henry turn and set off along the path, running as fast as his legs would carry him towards the entrance to the park.

Over on the island, Albert Hollins looked around and took stock of his surroundings.

On close inspection, the island proved to be

slightly bigger than it had seemed from the bank. There were, too, plenty of thick bushes and deep undergrowth in which to hide. Also, Albert discovered, there were a great many ducks – most of whom appeared none too pleased at sharing their island home with the hairy visitor. They quacked and squawked, complainingly, and flapped their wings in irritation.

Albert sought out for himself a quiet spot inside some bushes. He sat down, squeezed as much water as he could from his trouser-bottoms and then slipped on his socks again. Glancing through the branches across the lake, he saw that he had made the crossing only just in time. Already, there were people wandering, in twos and threes, along the path. An old man in a belted raincoat was sitting on the park bench, splitting an orange into segments and laying them, neatly, on a newspaper he had put down beside him. A small boy in a green sweater and patched jeans was standing on the bank, gazing out towards the island.

Albert Hollins put his arms round his knees and hunched down out of sight. "A fine Diamond-Days weekend this is turning out to be," he grumbled to himself. "I've turned into a horrible hairy monster, I'm soaked to the skin ... I'll either come down with the flu or end up on public show in a menagerie!" Albert's eyes narrowed as the grey-green duck with the bright orange beak pushed its way through the long grass and waddled into his hiding-place.

"Qua-a-*a-ack*!" squawked the duck, angrily.

"Shove off!" grunted Albert.

The duck left.

Albert Hollins sighed, tried to ease his body into a more comfortable position, and settled down for a long wait.

5

"This is most definitely the life!" said Detective-Sergeant Leslie Cooney, screwing up a toffee-paper and flicking it out of the police-car window. Then, putting his hands behind his head and leaning back in his seat, he added, "What do you say, Constable Poole?"

Detective-Constable Ernest Poole, at the wheel of the car, shrugged. "Not bad, Sergeant," he said. "But I wouldn't have minded being in uniform and on duty at Upton Park this afternoon – it's the big match today: West Ham versus Spurs."

"You don't know when you're well off, Poole," snapped the detective-sergeant, coldly. "Look out there," he added, nodding out of the window. "You couldn't have it nicer than that."

They were travelling down Regent Street. It was quite early in the afternoon. The pavements were thronged with sightseers and shoppers. There was not a hint of trouble anywhere.

"You don't, you know," continued Cooney, warming to his theme. "You don't know when you're in clover, Poole. Here we are, cruising round London in a comfy car, a nearly-full bottle of lemonade in the glove compartment, plenty of toffees to keep us going—" Detective-Sergeant Cooney paused long enough to pat his jacket and reassure himself that he hadn't been relieved of his bag of toffees by some pickpocket, and then went on, "and here's you asking to be flung into the hurly-burly world of football hooligans! No, Constable, this is where it's at – in the CID. Besides, when it's time for football, we can listen to it on the car radio."

"But it's not the same, is it, Sergeant?" argued Poole. "You don't get the atmosphere on the radio."

"*Atmosphere*!" sneered the detective-sergeant. "Stone the crows, Constable, have you forgotten what it was like at football matches, when you were in the uniformed branch? Getting your helmet knocked over your eyes? Having your toes stamped on? I tell you, Poole, you don't know when you're well off, lad—" He broke off as something caught his eye out of the car window. "Hello, hello, hello? He seems to be in a hurry," he continued, looking at a boy of about eleven years of age who was haring along the pavement, threading his way

79

between the passers-by, as if his very life depended on it. "You don't suppose he's robbed a bank, do you? Or planted a bomb underneath the Houses of Parliament?"

"Shall I pull over, Sarge?" asked Poole. "Do you want to question him?"

"It was a joke, you wally!" snapped Cooney, sourly. "Drive on!"

The police car picked up speed and turned left at Oxford Circus.

Henry Hollins, the boy running along Regent Street, had not seen the police car. What he *did* see though was a red London bus which, he felt sure, was going in his direction. As the bus pulled up at a stop, Henry sprinted the last few yards and jumped on to the platform.

"Does this bus go past the Hotel Emilion?" he panted, very much out of breath after all the running he had done since he had left St James's Park.

"It had better do, young man," said the conductor with a grin, "or else I shall chop the driver's tail off!"

Henry sighed with relief and clambered up to the top deck.

Reggie Perkins, back on duty at his hall porter's desk, set out his pencils, his ballpoint pens, his memo pad, and his souvenir eraser shaped like a London taxi cab in a neat and orderly pattern on his blotter. As he did so, Reggie hummed along cheerfully to the background Muzak playing in the hotel's foyer.

Reggie Perkins much preferred his duties as a hotel porter to those of being a temporary waiter. As a hotel porter he was, to some extent, his own boss. He was in control of things. He was Monarch-of-All-That-He-Surveyed . . .

"Good afternoon, Reggie," said a voice at his elbow, causing him to jump a little. "Can I give you my room-key – I'm just going out."

"Sorry, Deborah," said Perkins, who had not noticed her arrival. "I was miles away, I'm afraid." He took the key from Debbie and put it in its little pigeon hole. He turned back to her with a smile. "Venturing out into the capital city, are you?" he said. "And what jetsetting high-life excitements have you got lined up for yourself this lunchtime? Cocktails at the Ritz, is it, with a debonair young Guards officer? Or wining and dining in some posh Mayfair restaurant with an aristocratic peer of the realm?"

"I wish it was, Reggie!" replied Debbie, with a grin. "I'd settle for either of those! But it's nothing quite so exciting, I'm afraid. I've got to match up some wool for a cardie I'm knitting for my mum's birthday – oh, and then I promised Dad I'd ransack London for a pair of strong left-handed nail scissors so he can cut his toenails."

"Ah well, never mind," said Perkins, encouragingly. "P'raps you'll meet a debonair young Guards officer or a gadabout aristocratic peer of the realm next time you're down."

"Some hope!" said the pretty hostess, pulling a face.

"You never know your luck!" said the hall porter. Beckoning Debbie closer, he glanced up and down the hotel foyer to make sure that no one else was listening, and continued, "We've got our favourite VIP staying with us again. He's a real live Arabian prince, no less! One of your Gulf States lot – and a multi-millionaire to boot. He's loaded with cash. He's taken over an entire floor of the hotel, would you believe?"

"That's just the sort of chap I'm looking for," said Debbie, smiling. "You'll have to introduce me to him."

Perkins shook his head. "It wouldn't do you much good, Deborah, if I did. He's got fifty wives already. That's why he needs the whole fifth floor for elbow room."

"*Fifty*?" gasped the hostess. Then she shrugged. "Oh well, there's no point in me building up my hopes then."

"Not unless you fancy being number fifty-one," said Perkins, with a grin.

"No, thank you very much. I'll keep my mind on knitting wool and toenail clippers." Debbie glanced at her watch. "Just look at the *time*! If I stand here yacking to you any longer, I'm not going to get my shopping done. Have a nice afternoon, Reggie!"

"Take care, Deborah!"

Perkins watched, appreciatively, as the hostess's trim figure tripped across the foyer and went out through the revolving doors. They had only just stopped revolving on Debbie when they spun round again and Henry Hollins entered, having just got off the bus.

"Hello, young Henry," said Perkins, as the boy hurried up to the porter's desk. "I thought you and your dad were out seeing the sights? Do you want your room-key?"

"No, thanks, Mr Perkins," said Henry. "It's you that I've come back to see."

"What is it, son?" asked Perkins, noting the anxiety in Henry's voice.

"It's about Dad, Mr Perkins."

"Why – what's wrong with him?"

"He's . . . Can you keep a secret, Mr Perkins?"

Perkins drew himself up to his full height and puffed out his chest. "I'm a hotel porter, Henry," he said, importantly. "If *I* can't be trusted with a secret – I'd like to know who can!"

Henry glanced up and down the hotel lobby. Apart from the receptionist who was sitting behind her counter munching a Mars Bar and reading a romantic novel, there was not a soul in sight. All the same, Henry took no chances. He leaned over the porter's desk and spoke to Perkins in a whisper.

"It's . . . It's Dad, Mr Perkins – he's . . . he's changed into a horrible hairy monster."

The hotel porter let out a long low whistle through his teeth. "No!" he murmured, stunned by this news. "I can't believe it! He's such a quiet, amiable sort of chap!" Perkins frowned and spoke sternly. "You're not pulling my leg, I hope, young Henry?"

Henry Hollins shook his head. "I wouldn't, Mr Perkins – not about a thing like that."

Perkins held Henry's unblinking gaze for several seconds. "I believe you, Henry," he said, at last. "And you're sure there hasn't been some sort of mistake?"

Henry shook his head again, as firmly as before. "I only wish there had."

"But *how*?" asked the porter. "Where? *When*?"

"It all began last night," began Henry, launching into his story. "It was all because of that doctor he went to see about his back."

"Not the one I recommended to you, I hope?"

"The one called Doctor Jekyll, yes."

"Oh, dear me."

"But it wasn't your fault, Mr Perkins," said Henry, quickly. "In fact, it wasn't even the doctor's fault – it was a mix-up over some prescriptions. Dad took the wrong one. When he drank the medicine, it turned him into Mr Hyde."

"Well, I never!" said Perkins, raising his eyebrows. "What a funny carry-on! I've heard of some strange things in my time, Henry, but I've never come across anything like this before. Where is your dad?"

"He's hiding in some bushes on a little island in St James's Park. I had to leave him there while I came back here, Mr Perkins." Henry looked up into the hall porter's face, beseechingly. "Will you come with me and help rescue him?"

"I'm afraid I can't, Henry," said Perkins, with a shake of his head. "Not at this immediate moment at any rate – I'm on duty. It's more than my job is worth to leave this desk. Does your mother know what's happened to your dad?"

"No! And she mustn't find out, neither. I promised him I wouldn't tell her."

"Then you'd best make yourself scarce, lad," whispered Perkins. "Here she comes!"

The lift doors along the foyer had just opened and Emily Hollins, having stepped out, was heading

straight for the porter's desk. Luckily, Henry was hidden from his mother's view by a huge potted plant that stood directly between them – but in a second she would be sure to spot him.

"Quick, lad!" said Perkins. As he spoke, he grabbed Henry by the shoulder, whisked him round behind the desk and pushed him down out of sight.

Just in time!

"I'm sorry to be a bother," said Emily Hollins, as she walked up to Perkins with an apologetic smile. "But I don't suppose you've seen anything of my husband or my son?"

Perkins, who happened to have his right hand resting on Henry Hollins's head at that very moment, crossed the fingers of his left hand behind his back and cleared his throat. "I'm afraid not, Mrs Hollins," he fibbed. "Why? Have you lost them?"

Emily nodded. "They were supposed to meet me here for lunch," she said. "I can't think where they've got to."

"I'm sure they'll turn up soon," said Perkins. "I'll tell you what – while you're waiting, why don't you try the Hotel Emilion's famous Street-Sellers of Old London Coffee Shop? You'll like it in there – it's got pictures of all the old street-hawkers of long ago painted round the walls. Muffin men and lavender ladies and so forth. You could have a cup of coffee while you're taking in the murals."

"That sounds nice!" said Emily.

Underneath the hall porter's desk, Henry Hollins let out a sigh of relief.

"Just down the foyer and turn left at our famous Landmarks of Old London Grill Room and Restaurant," said Perkins. Then: "It's all right, Henry, panic over," he continued once Mrs Hollins had moved out of sight.

"But what am I going to do about Dad?" said Henry, after he had crept out from his hiding place.

"Listen, Henry," said the hall porter, "I don't like to think of your mum sitting in that coffee shop on her own, while your dad's stuck out there on that island, all hairy and horrible. And I *do* feel responsible in some small way. After all, it *was* me that sent you to that doctor. I'll do everything I can to help – what is it you want?"

"Have you got a car, Mr Perkins?"

"I've got the Escort, yes," said Perkins, "but—"

"If we could just go back there, wait until it's quiet, and then fetch Dad back to the hotel – he can't walk through the streets, you see, looking like he does at the moment, and I don't think that they'd let him on a bus. He'd frighten the other passengers."

"I was about to say, Henry, that I've got the Escort, yes, but what I haven't got is any petrol in the tank."

"Can't we buy some petrol?"

Perkins shook his head, ruefully. "The fact of the matter is, Henry, I'm skint – flat broke," he said with a shrug. "I'm afraid your problem has caught me too close to the end of the month. I don't get paid until next week. I'd borrow a few pounds, but the rest of the hotel staff are in the same embarrassing predicament."

Henry dug his hands deep down into his own empty pockets, then bit his lip, anxiously. "But if we don't do *something* quickly, Mr Perkins, that park's going to be full of people," he said. "And then somebody's bound to spot him – it's only a titchy little island."

The hotel porter wrinkled his brow as he thought hard and his eyes narrowed as something else caught his attention.

"Give me five minutes, Henry," said Perkins, nodding along the hotel foyer. "I mustn't neglect His Royal Highness."

Henry followed Perkins's glance and and saw a tall, proud-looking Arab in snowy-white flowing robes and head-dress coming down the ornate staircase. Behind the Arab walked a great many Arabic ladies, all wearing equally spotless white linen robes, their faces hidden behind their yash-maks as they chattered to one another, excitedly.

"Who are they all, Mr Perkins?" asked Henry, curious.

"He's the Hotel Emilion's best ever customer, lad," whispered the hall porter. "Prince Achmed of Barania. His country's *swimming* in oil. He could *bath* in it if he wanted to – except that would probably make him mucky. And those are all his lady wives that he's got with him."

"Wow!" said Henry, impressed.

"Look, Henry. You nip over and have a look at the paperbacks on the hotel's bookstand outside the newspaper stall – I'll be with you as soon as I've attended to His Highness's wants."

Henry did as he was told and took himself across the hotel's foyer where he watched from behind the revolving bookstand as the prince and his party of wives approached the porter's desk.

"Yes, Your Royal Highness, what's your problem?" asked Perkins, having to raise his voice above the constant chattering of the prince's wives. "And what's more important," he continued obligingly, "what can I do to help?"

"Oh amiable Perkins, may mighty Allah take pity on me!" sighed Prince Achmed. "Surely it is written, is it not, that a prince in London with fifty wives is like unto a blind camel-master whose herd is scattered across the desert sand?"

"If it isn't written, Your Highness, then it jolly well should be," replied the hotel porter, hiding a smile. "Although, speaking personally, you have me at somewhat of a disadvantage – me being a single gentleman with neither wife nor camel to my name. Camel, indeed!" he added with a chuckle. "Why – my landlady, Mrs Purvis, goes through the roof if I even mention keeping a kitten as a pet. But all this is hardly solving your problem – what's amiss?"

Prince Achmed let out another long, sad sigh and shook his head. "To put it into a . . . how do you say . . . a coconut husk?"

"I believe Your Highness means a nutshell," suggested Perkins.

"Aye, verily, to put the matter into a nutshell, my problem is as thus, oh venerable Perkins: one half of my harem wishes to pay a cultural visit to your excellent Windsor Castle; the other twenty-five of my wives are desirous of witnessing Tottenham Hotspurs play West Ham. There is an air-conditioned coach at their disposal but, in the name of Allah, I cannot chop the vehicle in half!"

The hotel porter sucked at the end of his pencil deep in thought for several seconds and then tapped it on his desk. "Leave it to me, Your Highness," he said at last. "I'll have a word with our doorman, Rayburn, and get something sorted out for you." Then, peering over the top of his desk and looking down towards the entrance, he bellowed at the top of his voice, "Mr Rayburn!"

Rayburn, the doorman, who sported a bristling military moustache and wore a smart, gold-braided cap, paused in the act of helping in an American tourist with his luggage. "Yes, Mr Perkins?" he called back.

"What's the latest word on His Highness's air-conditioned coach?"

"It's out on the hotel forecourt now, Mr Perkins. Sopwith, the driver, is having a lemon tea and a

Danish pastry in the Street-Sellers of Old London Coffee Shop – he's sitting under the mural of the Hot-Chestnut Man."

"I wonder if you would be so kind," said Perkins, "as to poke your head inside and tell him that the coach won't be needed this afternoon."

"*Not needed*, Mr Perkins?" said Rayburn, in some surprise.

"Not needed?" echoed Prince Achmed, equally astonished. "But—"

"Never fear, Your Royal Highness, I know exactly what I'm doing," said the hotel porter, and then raising his voice again he called out to the doorman, "Inform Sopwith that he's got the afternoon off and as soon as he gets his vehicle off the forecourt, call up a dozen black cabs from the rank."

"A d-d-d-dozen taxis?" stammered the Emilion's doorman. "What – all at one go?"

"Kindly do as I say, please, Mr Rayburn – and chop-chop about it!" said Perkins, firmly. Although many years younger than the doorman, the hotel porter had spent a longer time in the hotel's employ and therefore felt that he could order his junior associate about if necessary.

"Very good, Mr Perkins," snapped the doorman, recognizing at once the authority in the porter's voice. "I'll see to it immediately." Then, snapping his fingers at a porter to take over the handling of the American tourist's luggage, Rayburn shot off in the direction of the coffee shop.

Perkins smiled to himself, tapped his pencil against his teeth as he watched the doorman disappear, then turned back to Prince Achmed. "How's that, Your Royal Highness? You can load twenty-five of your good ladies into half a dozen taxis and shoot them out to Windsor via the motorway; while the other six cabs convey the rest of them to Upton Park to see the game."

"Allah be praised, Perkins!" cried the prince, clapping a hand to his brow. "Verily, you have the wisdom of Solomon! May the Prophet heap rewards in plenty upon your head – and may you one day sit upon his right hand." Then, slipping his hand inside his robes, he drew out a thick roll of banknotes, peeled one off and slipped it into Perkins' open hand, adding, "Meanwhile, accept this small gratuity with my unbounded thanks."

"Thank *you*, Your Royal Highness," replied Perkins, touching his forehead.

"All done and dusted," cried the doorman, Rayburn, as he sped back from the coffee shop. "Mr Sopwith's gone to move the coach and I'll have the first half dozen taxis on parade and ticking over in less than a jiffy."

"Well done, Rayburn!" called out Perkins, who

was always as quick to praise as he was to criticize. "Carry on with the good work!"

Rayburn paused and frowned as he approached the revolving door at the hotel's front entrance. "It looks to me as if I'm going to need that big black umbrella," he shouted back across the foyer. "By the look of that sky, we're in for a downpour!"

Perkins nodded in agreement. Looking down towards the entrance, he could see that outside it had suddenly grown dark and heavily overcast.

Prince Achmed was hastily ushering his party of wives towards the door, hoping to get them safely in their taxis before the heavens opened up.

"Over here, lad – quick!" Perkins beckoned Henry to join him.

"What is it, Mr Perkins?" asked Henry Hollins, hurrying across from the bookstand.

"Transport problem solved, Henry!" said Perkins, and he waved a crisp banknote in the air. "Look at what His Royal Nibs has just bunged me – a whole tenner, would you believe! I'm off duty too now," he added, glancing up at the large clock above the reception desk. "As soon as we've got some petrol in the Escort's tank, we'll see what's to be done about your father's bit of bother." He paused, as the entire foyer was suddenly lit up by a flash of lightning, followed almost immediately by an ear-splitting roll of thunder. The storm, it seemed, was only seconds away. "The sooner we get your dad safely off that island the better," pronounced Perkins. "Otherwise he's going to get soaked through."

6

Police-Constable Timothy Stiggins stared out gloomily through the trees from the shelter of the bandstand at the sheeting rain. "Just my luck!" he muttered to himself. "Trust me to be on duty in St James's Park when it's chucking it down!"

The fresh-faced, keen-eyed young policeman was normally a cheerful soul with a warm smile and a helpful disposition. He was always ready to give a passer-by the correct time and ever quick to assist any puzzled tourist seeking directions to the British Museum or the Tower of London. But this was not one of PC Stiggins's better days. He pushed his hands deep down in the pockets of his black serge trousers and sucked at his teeth in disgust.

It was not that Timmy Stiggins objected to patrolling the royal park – on the contrary, he delighted in the area, knowing every twist and turn of its meandering paths by heart. Neither was it that he disliked rain – quite the reverse: at home with his mum in Dulwich he was responsible for tending the garden and knew full well that, without the gentle gift of rain, the flowers would die and the grass would wither.

It was the combination of the location *and* the adverse weather that was really getting him down.

The truth of the matter was that the young PC was a nature-lover and an avid bird-watcher. Normally, there were ample opportunities for Stiggins to combine duty with pleasure and pursue his hobby while patrolling his beat in the park. But not when it was raining cats and dogs.

Bird-watching is, principally, a fair weather pastime. On any fine day, in his off-duty hours, every spare moment of the young constable's time was spent out in the countryside, cheese-and-Marmite sandwiches and flask of tea in his rucksack, binoculars held tight to his face, blissfully observing his feathered friends: watching a Blackcap Warbler, perhaps, building its nest in a bramble hedge; listening to the "chuck-chuck" of a Wheater which had paused in its migratory flight to the northern moors, having come all the way from Africa; or even, maybe, sighting a Lesser Spotted Woodpecker in some spinney, drumming away in its search for insects high up on the trunk of an oak tree.

Bird-watching on his beat, of course, was a different affair: house sparrows and wrens mostly, but with the occasional sighting of a chaffinch calling out its familiar cry of "pink-pink" in somebody's back garden.

But St James's Park was another story again. It was in the park, down by the lake, that Constable Stiggins liked to watch the ducks and the dabchicks and the moorhens and the swans.

Timothy Stiggins smiled fondly to himself as he recalled a green-headed mallard drake he had befriended on his last visit to the park. The cheeky creature had waddled out of the lake right up to where he knelt and had taken a piece of stale Dundee cake off the palm of his hand. And how the onlookers had cheered!

Officially, going by the Metropolitan Policeman's Code, he was not supposed to carry stale Dundee cake in his uniform pockets – they were reserved for whistles, notebooks, pencils and such. His station sergeant would have had the screaming blue-abdabs had he known about the titbits that the young police constable carried about his person for his feathered friends.

"But what the eye doesn't see," Stiggins told himself, "the heart doesn't grieve over."

Timothy Stiggins smiled again in fond recollection, then patted the left-hand side of his tunic. Through the pocket he could feel the bulge of the brown paper bag containing the remains of a strawberry-jam-filled sponge cake left over from the previous Sunday's afternoon tea. His little friend, the mallard drake, would appreciate some stale cake crumbs.

"Oh, blow the wet!" Stiggins said out loud, and he straightaway stepped out from underneath the bandstand's shelter to set off through the trees towards the lake. His mind made up and anxious to see the ducks, he barely noticed the huge droplets of rain that bounced off the overhead leaves, splashed on to his helmet, rolled off and dribbled down the back of his neck.

There *was* one good thing to be said for the rain, the constable told himself: at least it would keep the public out of the park. He could count on having the lake and its feathered occupants to himself – and that was far and away the best situation for bird-watching.

Sure enough, when he arrived on the path that skirted the lake, there was not another human being in sight. Plenty of duck and other water birds, though, were swimming around on the lake in the pouring rain without a care in the world.

Police-Constable Stiggins peered all around for a sighting of the friendly mallard. "Here, drake!" he called. "Here, drake, drake, drake, drakie!" But his special friend was nowhere to be seen. Stiggins put his hand to his forehead to shield his eyes from the driving rain and peered across the lake towards the little island in the middle.

Over on the island, lying low in the undergrowth out of sight, cold and cramped and soaking wet, Albert Hollins shivered and glowered at the ducks that waddled all around him, angrily quacking their complaints at the trespasser on their rightful domain.

"Oh, do shut up, ducks – *do*!" growled Albert, in his new strange-sounding Edward-Hyde voice. "It's bad enough being stuck out here, soaked to the skin, with pins and needles, *and* catching my death of cold, as like as not – without you lot putting your two-pennyworth in." Mr Hollins wriggled uneasily on the wet grass, and added, "Where on earth have you got to, Henry? Do get a move on, son!"

Then, in his anxiety, he raised his head and peered across the water towards the lakeside path. He looked straight into the face of the young policeman standing on the bank.

"Fizzing heckers!" muttered Albert to himself, immediately ducking down again.

But it was too late.

The damage had been done.

Over on the path, Police-Constable Timothy Stiggins swallowed twice, blinked hard, and then swallowed again. He had just set eyes on the face of the ugliest thing he had ever seen in his life.

Whatever it was, it was now out of sight. But there was not a shadow of doubt in the young policeman's mind that he *had* seen it. His eyes had not deceived him. He was, after all, a fully trained member of the Metropolitan Police Force, highly skilled in the art of memorising photographically everything he saw. And the face that he had just stared into, he told himself, was not the face of an ordinary human being – it was the face of a horrible hairy monster!

Police-Constable Stiggins did not panic. He knew exactly what to do – keep calm, at all costs. His hand, trembling slightly, shot up to the little two-way radio attached to his tunic lapel and switched it on.

"Alpha Bravo Foxtrot calling Charlie Echo Leader," he snapped into the microphone. Then, without taking his eyes from the patch of grass out on the island where he had looked into the horrible face of the intruder, he switched the radio to "receive".

"Charlie Echo Leader here!" the voice of his station sergeant crackled out at him. "Receiving you loud and clear, Alpha Bravo Foxtrot – state your position – over!"

Police-Constable Stiggins switched his radio back to "send". "I am standing on the path beside the lake in St James's Park, Sergeant," he began, trying hard not to sound as nervous as he felt, "and there's nobody about because it's pelting down with rain . . . and, oh Sarge, you're not going to believe me when I tell you what I've just seen . . . over!"

"Try me, Alpha Bravo Foxtrot," replied the calm and reassuring voice at the other end, adding, "Over!"

The young police constable took a very deep breath, swallowed hard, and then launched into his story . . .

The windscreen wipers whipped to and fro at full speed as the Ford Escort crawled at a snail's pace along Buckingham Palace Road in the driving rain.

"Can't we go any faster, Mr Perkins?" said Henry Hollins, glumly.

"I'm afraid not, lad," replied the hotel porter, shaking his head and nodding at the long line of almost stationary cars stretched ahead of them. "Not in this traffic. It's the bad weather, d'y'see – it creates havoc on the roads."

"If Dad's still sitting on that island, he'll be wet through – he'll probably get double pneumonia."

"I appreciate his problem, Henry, believe me – I only wish there was something I could do. There is one good thing to be said for this weather though – at least it'll keep the crowds out of St James's Park. It isn't likely anybody's going to spot your—"

The hotel porter broke off at the urgent wail of a fast-approaching siren.

"What is it, Mr Perkins?" asked Henry as the noise increased. "Is it an ambulance?"

"No, Henry – a police car, by the sound of it," said Perkins. "More delay, I'm afraid," he added with a sigh as he swung the steering wheel and guided the Escort into the kerb to allow the vehicle to pass.

"Which way is it going?" asked Henry.

"The very same direction that we're headed for ourselves, lad," replied the hotel porter as the police car shot past at speed, its siren blaring and the blue warning light flashing on the roof. "Straight towards Buckingham Palace and St James's Park."

An awful thought occurred to Henry. "Mr Perkins," he began, "you don't suppose, do you, that the police have found out about . . ." His voice trailed off – the possibility was too dreadful for him to contemplate.

"I don't know *what* to think, Henry," said Perkins, not wanting to admit to his young passenger that the very same thought *had* occurred to him. "I'll say this much though – wherever that police car's going, *we're* stopping put – this traffic jam is absolutely *solid*!"

Henry Hollins blinked, let out a long, sad sigh and stared solemnly at the pouring rain as it rattled down on the bonnet of the car and bounced in the puddles along the road.

Albert Hollins, lying low in the thick undergrowth on the island, shivered, sneezed, then twitched with fear when he heard the strident sound of the siren as the police car turned into the park and hurtled down the path towards the lake.

Albert's heart sank into his boots. "Oh, heckers," he groaned to himself, "that copper must have spotted me and radioed for reinforcements – *now* what do I do?" But there was very little that he *could* do – except press his body close to the earth and hope against hope that this latest problem would go away.

Hugging the ground beneath him, however, presented an entirely new problem. The island, as he had already had cause to discover, was covered with years of accumulated duck-dirt. The filthy smelly stuff stuck to his suit, his socks, his shirt and, what was even more distasteful, it was now all over his hands and wrists. Pressing his face close to the ground brought his nose in direct contact with the disgusting substance.

"Pooh!" said Albert, unhappily. "I not only *look* horrible – I even *smell* horrible as well!"

On the lakeside path, the police car pulled up sharply as the brakes were slammed on hard.

The two front doors opened simultaneously as the occupants of the vehicle leapt out into the still pouring rain.

"Where is it, Constable Poole?" said Detective-Sergeant Cooney, peering across the lake. "Can you see anything?"

"I can see the little island, Sergeant, with all the ducks on it," replied Detective-Constable Poole. "Bless my soul, Sarge!" he continued with delight. "Can you see that orangey-browney duck in the bushes? Isn't it pretty?"

"Never mind the fizzing ducks, Poole!" snapped Cooney. "We're here to apprehend a horrible hairy monster – if our information is correct and not some kind of hoax. And speaking of that information – where's the uniformed copper that's supposed to have radioed it in?"

"Here comes one of the uniformed branch now, Sarge," said Poole, pointing through the trees along the path.

Police-Constable Stiggins was charging through the undergrowth towards the two plain-clothes men. He had remained in hiding ever since first sighting the monster, and there were bits of branches and wet leaves attached to his sopping wet uniform.

"Stone me, Poole – he's an unlikely looking specimen," sniffed Cooney, as the uniformed constable approached them at full speed, leaping over flower beds and bushes. "If he's dragged us down here on some wild goose chase, there'll be serious trouble."

Constable Stiggins arrived out of breath and panting heavily. He skidded on the path and pulled himself up short in front of Detective-Sergeant Cooney. Then, bringing himself smartly to attention, he slammed his right foot down hard in a puddle and succeeded in splashing the lower half of Cooney's trousers.

Detective-Sergeant Cooney frowned. "Are you Police-Constable Stiggins?" he asked.

"That's me, Sergeant."

The rain was coming down unceasingly on Detective-Sergeant Cooney's recently purchased dove grey sports jacket. This was no way, he told himself, to spend a Saturday afternoon. "Do you want to tell us what you saw, lad, and be quick about it," he said aloud. "We don't want to be stuck out here in this weather any longer than needs be."

"Righty-ho, Sarge," said Stiggins, unbuttoning his tunic-pocket. "I'll just consult my notebook – make sure I've got my facts straight." He flipped the notebook open at the relevant page, cleared his throat and then began to read. "Whilst proceeding through St James's Park, on my appointed beat, creeping quietly through the trees, all at once—"

"Just a minute, Stiggins," broke in Detective-

Sergeant Cooney. "Hold your horses, lad – there's something rather fishy in what you just said."

"Fishy, sergeant?" replied Stiggins, nervously.

"You heard me, lad – fishy. Distinctly odd. What were you doing creeping about in the trees, if you were supposed to be on your beat? Coppers on their beat are not supposed to creep about – they're expected to keep themselves smart and upright and go about their duties in a policeman-like manner. Were you expecting to see a horrible hairy monster on that island?"

Police-Constable Stiggins blinked. He realized that he had said too much. The only thing to do now was to own up. "No, Sarge – 'course not," he said, and then paused for a moment to summon up his courage and blurt out the truth. "The fact is, I'm a bit of an ornithologist on the side."

"No!" exclaimed Detective-Constable Poole. "Are you really, Constable?"

Stiggins glanced down at the ground, modestly, and shuffled the toe of his boot in the gravel on the path. "Yeah – y'know – just a hobby."

"Brill!" said Detective-Constable Poole, very much impressed and then, turning to Detective-Sergeant Cooney, he went on to explain, "An ornithologist's a bird watcher, Sergeant."

"I know very well what an ornithorni-what's-its-name is, Poole!" lied the Detective-Sergeant.

"Kindly keep out of this." Then, turning back to Stiggins, he added, "Carry on, Constable."

"Well, Sergeant, as there was nobody in the park – what with all this rain – I thought I'd keep out of sight, behind the trees, and study a few ducks."

"What?" said Cooney, sourly. "On duty?"

Constable Stiggins decided to ignore this latest sarcasm and his eyes went back to the notes he had compiled.

"Whilst proceeding on my beat, creeping quietly through the trees—" he began again.

"Never mind what's written down in your notebook, Constable Stiggins!" snapped Detective-Sergeant Cooney. "I want to hear it from your lips exactly the way it was! Does your station-sergeant know that you spend your time playing with the ducks?"

"I don't play with them, Sergeant," replied Timothy Stiggins stoutly. "I watch them. I observe their feeding habits and that. And I don't neglect my duties neither – I carry them out to the last letter. It's just that, as I move along, I also keep my eyes peeled for anything special that might be happening in the world of our feathered friends."

"Hey, Stiggo!" cried Constable Poole, excitedly. "Did you happen to spot that orangey-brown duck out on the island – it's a little cracker!"

"Oh, yes," replied Stiggins. "I've seen it dozens of times – although strictly speaking, Constable . . ." He broke off and frowned as it suddenly occurred to him that he didn't know the name of his new-found friend. "What do they call you?" he asked.

"Ernest. Ernest Poole – but all my chums call me Ernie."

"Well then, strictly speaking, Ernie, that orangey-brown duck you were referring to is more in the nature of being a drake."

"How on earth can you possibly tell at this distance?" gasped Constable Poole in amazement, screwing up his eyes and peering across the water.

"Easy-peasy," said Stiggins, knowledgeably. "You may find this hard to believe, Ernie, but in the world of our feathered friends, it's the male of the species that's the more colourful—"

"Will you two pack it in!" snapped Detective-Sergeant Cooney, angrily. "I'm standing here get-ting soaked to the skin while you pair of nature lovers witter on about the fizzing wildlife! We're supposed to be here to nab a horrible hairy monster." He broke off to shake the rain from his hair and pull his soaking wet coat collar up round his ears. "Look," he went on, "let's get back inside the car for a start – at least it's dry in there and we can figure out our next move in comfort."

The suggestion seemed a sound one and Poole

and Stiggins followed Detective-Sergeant Cooney into the police car. They all three scrambled into the back seat with Cooney sitting in the middle.

"That's more like it," said Cooney, shuffling his bottom to and fro on the seat so that he had the most room. "Now then, Constable Stiggins – tell us all about this monster you think you saw!"

"But I did see it, Sarge!" protested the uniformed constable. "I'm a trained bird-watcher, remember – my eyes don't play tricks on me."

"Get on with it, lad," said Cooney. "But I warn you – if you so much as mention the word 'ducks' again, or 'bird-watching', I shall come down on you like a ton of bricks."

"Like I said, Sergeant, the monster's over on that island," said Stiggins, nodding across the water through the car's rear window. "I spotted him while I was watching the . . ." He paused, remembering Cooney's warning about the words that he was not supposed to use. ". . . While I was watching the things with beaks and covered in feathers," he concluded, lamely.

"Go on," said Cooney.

"That's all there is to tell, Sergeant," replied Stiggins with a shrug. "The monster only popped its head up for a second – but it was more than long enough for me, I can tell you – all covered in hair, it was, and with this sort of wrinkled face – it was horrible, Sergeant, horrible . . . *Urgh*!" Constable Stiggins shivered at the awful memory.

"Are you sure you've got your facts straight, Constable?" demanded Cooney, not at all convinced by Stiggins's story.

Constable Stiggins licked his forefinger and held it up for the detective-sergeant's inspection. "See this wet, see this dry, slit my throat if I tell a lie," he said. "I'm positive, Sarge. It was the same one time when I was in the Lake District and I *knew* I'd spotted a Great-Crested Warble-Hammer and everybody tried to tell me it was only a Yellow-Throated Missel-Thrush—"

Detective-Sergeant Cooney held up a warning finger. "What did I say, Stiggins, about bird-watching talk?" he said.

"Sorry, Sergeant – I got carried away. But I *did* see a monster on that island – and more than just the once – three or four times in all – there was one time when it stood right up and tried to shake the rain off itself."

"I only hope, for your sake, Stiggins," said Cooney, sternly, "that you're not trying to pull my leg."

"Of course not, Sergeant – I wouldn't."

Detective-Sergeant Cooney thought hard for a moment. The uniformed constable didn't look like the sort of policeman who told whoppers. Quite the reverse, in fact – he looked like a trustworthy sort of chap.

"Detective-Constable Poole!" he said. "I want you to keep your eyes fixed firmly on that island – and don't take them off it for an instant, right?"

"I can't, Sarge," announced the detective-constable.

Cooney scowled and pursed his lips. "Can't, Poole, lad?" he snarled. "*Can't*! There's no such word as 'can't', lad!"

"I mean, I can't see out of the rear window, Sarge – it's all steamed up," said Poole, nodding at the glass.

"Then wipe it clean with your sleeve, lad," Cooney growled. "Good heavens above! What else do you think they put sleeves on jackets *for*?"

Detective-Constable Poole did as his sergeant told him and applied the cuff of his jacket to the car window. He rubbed hard. Seconds later, the glass was crystal clear – and Poole's sleeve which had been wet before from the driving rain was now wetter still.

"That's better," said Cooney. "Now, constable, I want you to commence your surveillance of that island. If there *is* a monster on it, we'll nobble the beast – even if it means sitting here all day."

And so Detective-Sergeant Leslie Cooney, Detective-Constable Ernest Poole and Police-Constable Timothy Stiggins (uniformed branch), settled down on the back seat of the police car for what might prove to be a long vigil by the lakeside.

Cooney took the bag of toffees from his jacket pocket and passed them round. "See that you put your toffee papers in the ashtrays, not on the floor," he warned.

Moments later, there was no sound in the police car save for the noise of the policemen sucking on their toffees.

Over on the little island, the unhappy hairy and horrible-looking Albert Hollins shifted himself uncomfortably on the sodden undergrowth that was stained and slimy with duck-dirt.

The island's feathered inhabitants, accustomed now to Albert's presence, waddled all around and sometimes even over him in the hope, perhaps, that he might have a few cake crumbs or stale bits of bread about his person.

"Get off me, ducks!" snapped Albert. Then, raising his head no more than was necessary, he peered through the grass and across the water towards the parked police car which showed no sign of moving on. "Flippin' Nora!" growled Albert to himself. "How long are they intending to hang about? I've got cramp in my back, pins and needles in my right shoulder, my left big toe's gone to sleep

113

and, on top of all that, I'm covered in duck-dirt! *Yerks*!"

But there was nothing to be done – except lie low and wait . . .

7

Henry Hollins fidgeted on his seat, impatiently, as the Ford Escort crawled along in the pouring rain and the endless stream of traffic. It seemed as if they had been travelling at the same snail's pace for several hours. In fact, it could not have been more than fifteen minutes.

"How much longer before we get to the park, Mr Perkins?" said Henry.

"Soon be there now, Henry," Perkins replied. "I don't know – one drop of rain and the whole of London comes to a standstill. It's as if, at the first sign of a downpour, the entire population jump into their cars and drive round and round, in circles, looking for a traffic jam."

"I only hope that Dad's all right," said Henry, anxiously. "I wonder if he's still waiting for us on that island?"

"From your description of him, lad, he's hardly in a position to have moved anywhere else – not by himself – not if he's all hairy and horrible. Anyway, it won't be long now before we find out," said Perkins, pausing to point towards the vast expanse of green they were approaching. "We're coming up to St James's Park. I can't take the car in, but I'll park up here by the side of the road."

The hotel porter swung the car out of the crawling stream of traffic and pulled in at the kerb.

"There's one good thing," said Henry, as he opened the door on the passenger side, "I think this rain's easing off at last."

The boy was right. The heavy downpour had now given way to a light but steady drizzle that pitter-pattered on to the road.

"This way, Henry!" cried Perkins, setting off across the soaking grass towards the fringe of trees. "I think the lake's in this direction."

"It is, Mr Perkins – I remember now!" Henry shouted, joyfully. "It's down there – and I can see the island too . . ." But his voice trailed off and he gulped, then added sadly, "Oh, crumbs, Mr Perkins – that's done it!"

"What's the matter, Henry?"

"That police car – the one that zoomed past us when we were stuck in traffic – it *was* going after Dad – it's down there now, parked at the lakeside."

Perkins stared down through the trees to where his young companion was pointing. "You're right,

Henry," he said. "But at least that must mean they haven't nabbed your father yet – he must still be out there on the island, keeping his head down."

"What can we do to help him, Mr Perkins?"

Perkins was forced to shake his head and sigh. "Not a great deal, I'm afraid," he said. "At least, not at this particular moment. We don't want to tangle with the law, lad. If your father lies low and doesn't show himself, it's possible that they might get fed up of waiting and go away – the best thing we can do is keep out of sight and sit tight ourselves."

"Stay up here in the bushes, do you mean?" asked Henry.

"Well, either that or else . . ."

"Or else what, Mr Perkins?"

"We could go back and sit in the Escort, Henry. We could listen to the car radio for an hour or so – there's a big match on this afternoon at Upton Park. West Ham are playing at home to Tottenham Hotspurs. Prince Achmed, the Hotel Emilion's resident VIP, has got half his wives sitting in the stand. They're really looking forward to it – if you ask me, it'll be a right humdinger of a . . ."

Perkins did not finish. He could see from the look on Henry's face that the boy was too concerned about his dad's unfortunate predicament to want to listen to a football commentary on the car radio. "On second thoughts, Henry," continued Perkins,

"I think we'd better stay right where we are – and then, if anything does happen down there, we'll be on hand to deal with it."

Henry nodded, glumly.

There was nothing else to be done.

Henry Hollins and the hotel porter settled down inside a clump of rhododendron bushes. Their eyes were glued on the parked police car, awaiting events. Occasionally Henry glanced across at the island in the hope of catching a glimpse of his father.

Meanwhile, inside the police car, the two detectives and the police-constable were also waiting for something to happen.

"Any sign of it yet, Poole?" asked Detective-Sergeant Cooney.

"No, Sarge."

"I hope you're keeping your eyes peeled, lad," growled the detective-sergeant.

"I'm doing my best, Sergeant," replied Poole, "but the window still keeps steaming up – and it's getting very stuffy in here. My eyelids keep drooping – I keep wanting to drop off."

"Do you fancy a game of *I Spy With My Little Eye*?" asked Police-Constable Stiggins.

"No, Constable," said Cooney, coldly. "He does not want a game of *I Spy With My Little Eye*. Not unless it's something beginning with 'M' for

Monster and it's 'aitch' and 'aitch' for 'airy and 'orrible and it's over on that island!"

"I was only trying to think up ways of stopping Constable Poole from dropping off to sleep," explained Stiggins.

"Well, flippin' well don't," retorted Cooney. "I'll see to it that Poole keeps on his toes, Stiggins – and that goes for you as well if needs be! Now then, less of the chat and keep your eyes skinned for that monster, both of you."

"Right, Sarge!" snapped Stiggins and Poole in unison.

There was total silence in the police car and its three occupants settled down to continue their vigil – a silence that was broken only by the occasional rustle of toffee wrappers.

Over on the island, Albert Hollins was growing more and more uncomfortable. He was wet and cold and thoroughly miserable.

"It's no good, isn't this!" he croaked in the harsh and curious voice that came out of his mouth. "I shall have to move or I shall just go numb all over – and this filthy duck-muck on my hands pongs something rotten!"

He tried, at first, to ease his aching body without raising his head. But it was no use. He needed to raise himself and loosen the stiffness in his shoulders. He wanted, desperately, to wriggle his head to make the pain at the back of his eyes go away. But in order to do either of these things, it would be necessary for him to raise himself – and surely reveal his presence to the occupants of the police car on the mainland.

"Perhaps if I just lift up my head the teeniest-weeniest-twidgiest bit," he grunted, suiting his words with actions.

But the teeniest-weeniest-twidgiest bit proved the teeniest-weeniest-twidgiest bit too much.

"There it is again, Sarge!" cried Stiggins excitedly as Albert's monster face appeared for a moment on the island.

"He's right, Sarge!" exclaimed Poole, equally excited. "There is a monster, definitely. I saw it too that time!"

"Where?" demanded the detective-sergeant, who had not seen Albert for himself. Just as Mr Hollins had bobbed up over the undergrowth, Cooney had been intent on popping yet another toffee into his mouth without the other two noticing. Now he peered across the lake at the seemingly empty island. "There's nothing out there except blinkin' ducks," he grumbled.

"It's bobbed down again now, Sarge," said Poole, "But I got a really good look at it – and it's just like Stiggins said, Sarge – all this hair all over its face and really horrible looking. I mean really *really* horrible.

Detective-Sergeant Cooney pursed his lips, frowned, and stared hard into Poole's eyes. The detective-constable held his sergeant's gaze, unblinking. Poole was telling the truth. There was no doubt about that.

"All right," said Cooney. "Now we have established that there really is a monster, we know what steps we need to take, don't we?"

His two companions shook their heads and waited for Cooney to explain.

"It's obvious," snapped the detective-sergeant. "We've got to take that monster into custody."

Police-Constable Stiggins sucked in his breath.

Detective-Constable Poole raised his eyebrows. "Have we really, Sergeant?" he said, not relishing the task.

"Of course we have," replied Cooney. "The general public will be coming back into the park now that the rain's eased off – it's our duty to see that this place is safe for them to stroll about in. They don't come into St James's Park to have fizzing great monsters jumping up and grabbing them. Pass me that loud-hailer, Stiggins."

Constable Stiggins reached over and picked up the battery-powered loud-hailer from the front seat and handed it to Cooney.

"We'll give it a chance to surrender quietly first," said Cooney. He switched on the loud-hailer which crackled into life. Then, pointing it towards the island, the detective-sergeant bellowed into the mouth-piece, "You there! Monster! Over on the island—"

"Oh, stop it, stop it!" cried Constable Stiggins, clapping his hands over his ears.

"Give over, Sarge!" shouted Detective-Constable Poole, also covering up his ears.

"What's the matter with you two?" demanded Cooney, angrily.

"Wouldn't it be better, Sergeant," suggested Constable Stiggins, "if you opened the window first?"

All the police-car windows were shut tight and the sound of the loud-hailer had echoed and reverberated around the inside of the car, very nearly deafening the two constables.

"Wind down that window, Stiggins," said Cooney, gruffly. Then, poking the loud-hailer through the window, he began again. "You there! Monster! Over on the island! We know you're on there! We are members of the Metropolitan Police Force – we have the entire forces of New Scotland Yard at our disposal – we must warn you, monster, that we have you completely surrounded—"

"Are there more of us then, Sergeant?" asked Stiggins, eagerly.

Cooney placed a hand over the hailer's mouth-piece and glowered at the uniformed constable. "Of course there aren't any more of us, you ninny!" he growled. "I'm only saying that to fool him." Then, putting his mouth to the loud-hailer again, he shouted, "If you know what's good for you, my lad, you'll give yourself up now – before I send my men over there to fetch you in!"

Poole and Stiggins exchanged an anxious glance at this last remark, which did not go unnoticed by Cooney. "It's a *ruse*," he said to them. "I'm only pretending again. Heaven forbid that the nation's need and the call of duty might demand that you soft pair should get your socks wet!"

But ruse or not, the detective-sergeant's plan had worked.

Across on the island, Albert Hollins had listened to and digested every word.

"Oh, what's the use?" he muttered to himself, despondently. "I might just as well surrender, I suppose. I can't sit out here for ever, like Robinson bloomin' Crusoe—"

"Do you hear me over there?" Cooney's voice boomed out again across the water, causing several ducks to flutter their wings in fear. "I'm giving you one last chance. Stand up now. Raise your hairy hands above your horrible head – and then start wading back to shore! And if you haven't begun by the time I count to three, I'll send in these highly trained special assault police that I've got with me!"

"Crumbs," gasped Stiggins.

"Crikey," breathed Poole, and, "Does he mean us?"

"Is it still a ruse?" asked Stiggins.

"Still just pretend?" questioned Poole.

Cooney nodded at them both and then continued into the loud-hailer, "Starting now: One to be ready – two to be steady—"

"I'm coming!" cried Albert Hollins, pulling himself upright on his aching limbs. "Don't shoot! I'll do whatever you say – I give up!"

On the opposite bank, the three policemen clambered out of the police car to stare in amazement at the curious figure that gazed back at them.

"Stone the crows!" gasped Detective-Sergeant Cooney, as he looked at Albert Hollins for the very first time. "He is an ugly-looking customer and no mistake! I take it all back, Constable Stiggins, lad – you were quite right to summon our assistance in this matter. I've never come across anything quite so ugly in all my years as a detective!"

While all of this had been going on, Henry Hollins and Mr Perkins had been watching from the safety of the rhododendron bushes. Henry gulped as he saw his father, monster-face and all, lower himself off the island into the lake and then start wading back towards the shore.

Shoelaces knotted together and shoes slung round his neck; trousers rolled up around his hairy knees; and with his monster-face blinking solemnly up at the grey clouds still lurking overhead, Albert Hollins set off through the muddy water towards the three policemen waiting for him on the bank. Moments later he was clambering out.

"They've got him, Mr Perkins," said Henry Hollins, sadly, as his hairy-faced father was taken into custody.

The boy and the hotel porter watched helplessly as Albert Hollins was pushed on to the back seat of the police car, with Detective-Sergeant Cooney and Constable Stiggins sitting on either side of him.

"What will they do with him, Mr Perkins?" asked Henry as Detective-Constable Poole got into the driving seat and slammed the car door. "Will they lock him up?"

"I don't see how they can, Henry," said Mr Perkins, frowning. "It's not *his* fault he's a horrible hairy monster. To tell you the honest truth, lad, I don't know what they *can* do to him – but I'll tell you what *we're* going to do – come on!"

He pushed through the leafy rhododendron branches and set off at a speedy jog-trot across the wet grass towards the road and the parked Ford Escort.

"What *are* we going to do, Mr Perkins?" gasped Henry, panting as he tried to keep up with the hotel porter.

"Why – follow them, of course!" And so saying, Mr Perkins sped over the fringe of neatly trimmed grass that marked the edge of the park to the Escort.

"Get in, lad," he said, flinging open the car door. Just as they were both clambering into the Escort, they heard the urgent sound of the police-car's siren as the vehicle came out of the park.

Mr Perkins waited until the police car had moved past them before he started up the Escort's engine. "Seat belt, Henry," he instructed his young friend as he pulled the Escort out into the road and tucked it in behind the police car. "I shouldn't worry too much, lad," he continued, sympathetically, catching a glimpse of Henry's anxious face. "They won't keep your dad inside the police station for long – not once he's had a chance to explain to them who he is and how it all happened."

"But that's just it, Mr Perkins," replied Henry. "He *can't* tell them who he is."

"*Can't*?" echoed the hotel porter. "Why? Is he in some sort of trouble with the police already?"

"No – of course he isn't. What I mean, I suppose, is that he *won't* tell them who he is – wild horses wouldn't drag it out of him – in case it should get into the papers or on the telly and Mum should happen to find out. She'd go stark staring round the twist, would Mum, if she knew that Dad had turned into Mr Hyde, the horrible hairy monster."

The hotel porter shrugged his shoulders. "But she's bound to find out sooner or later, Henry," he protested. "I mean, she's *sure* to notice that he's turned all hairy and horrible when she comes face to face with him again. It's not the sort of thing that you can cover up. Besides, women have a funny habit of noticing things like that – my mum notices if I go without a shave until tea-time—" Perkins broke off to glance at his watch and then nodded towards the dashboard. "Could you do me a favour, Henry?" he asked.

"What's that, Mr Perkins?"

"Just lean forward and switch on the radio, would you? I don't want to take my eyes off that police car."

Henry's eyes widened. "You don't think that they'll have it on the news yet, do you, Mr Perkins? About Dad turning into a monster?"

"No, of course not, Henry. But it's just gone a quarter to four – they'll be broadcasting the half-time scores – I was wondering how West Ham were getting on."

Henry leaned forward and turned the switch on the car radio which was already tuned to Radio Two and the Saturday afternoon's sport.

"—Norwich City nil, Crystal Palace nil," intoned the smooth voice of the sports announcer who continued, "Portsmouth one, Sunderland nil – Shrewsbury Town nil, Charlton two—"

Meanwhile, ahead of the Ford Escort, at the wheel of the police car, Detective-Constable Poole had *his* car radio on and was listening intently to the very same programme.

"—Stoke City one, Oldham Athletic one – Wimbledon two, Manchester City nil – Liverpool seven—"

But before Poole could discover which soccer team had been the unlucky recipients of the seven first-half goals that Liverpool had stuck into their net, a hand reached over from behind and switched off the radio.

"Blow the half-time scores, Poole," said Cooney, whose hand it was. "We've more important things on our plate than football scores." The detective-sergeant turned and stared solidly into the face of the monster sitting next to him. "What about it, sunshine?" he went on. "Are you going to come clean and tell us who you are and where you come from?"

But there was no reply from the monster. Albert Hollins's sad eyes stared back at Cooney out of his hairy wrinkled face. His mouth stayed shut tight.

"It's no good, Sarge," said Constable Stiggins. "He isn't going to speak."

"He'll talk all right," snarled Cooney. "Once we get him to the station. I'll see to that." The detective-sergeant paused and smiled to himself. "You never know, Poole," he continued to his constable assistant at the wheel. "There could be an MBE in this for me – bringing in a horrible hairy monster."

"Do you think so, Sarge?" said Poole, casting a doubtful glance at his superior through the rear mirror.

Cooney preened himself and sucked thoughtfully on the last remaining bit of toffee. "I don't see why not," he said. "Good heavens above – they dish out

129

MBE medals for nothing these days. There was an old biddy in Accrington who got one just for standing for yonks behind the counter of a post office. If I don't deserve one for this little lot, I don't know who does." He paused and then tried saying it out loud to see what it would sound like, "Detective-Sergeant Leslie Cooney, MBE – yes, it's got a ring to it, has that." He peered across at Stiggins who was sitting on the other side of the monster, and added, "What do you think, Constable?"

Timothy Stiggins shrugged. If anyone deserved a medal, he thought, it was himself. After all, he was the one who had seen the monster in the first place. But he deemed it wiser to keep his true feelings to himself. "If you say so, Sergeant," he said, tactfully.

"I do say so, Constable," replied Cooney with a frown. Something was beginning to trouble him. He sniffed, then sniffed again. His frown increased and his eyebrows met above his nose as he wrinkled up his face. "Can you smell anything, Poole?" he asked.

"It's funny you should say that, Sarge," replied the detective-constable. "I keep thinking that I can. Something seems to keep wafting in this direction – but it seems to be coming from the back of the car, where you three are sitting."

Detective-Sergeant Cooney sniffed again – longer and deeper this time. He grimaced distastefully. "*Poooh*!" he cried. "It's getting worse! It's not coming from you, is it, Stiggins?"

"No, Sergeant!"

"Are you sure, lad? It isn't coming from your boots? You haven't trod in something in that park? Something that the Royal Corgies might have left behind while they were being taken walkies?"

"No, Sergeant!" repeated the uniformed constable, stoutly. "But I can smell it too."

"It's me," croaked Albert Hollins sadly, in his monster voice, finding his tongue at last. "It's duck-dirt." He held up his jacket sleeve for their inspection. "I was lying in it on that island. It's all up my sleeve and on my hand as well."

"Oh, crikey!" gasped Cooney as Mr Hollins's sleeve came closer to his nose and the smell grew stronger. "It's horrible!" he gasped, waving a hand in front of his face. Now that he knew what was causing the unpleasant smell, it seemed to him even worse than before. "Wind that window down – quick!" he said to Stiggins. "Hang his arm out of the window."

Timothy Stiggins reached for the window winder.

"Don't do that!" cried Detective-Constable Poole, glancing over his shoulder. "If you dangle his arm out of the window, everybody will think

I'm going to turn left all the time. We'll have an accident for sure!"

Detective-Sergeant Cooney was forced to agree. "All right," he said. "But you can wind the window down just the same, Stiggins – at least we can have some fresh air blowing through the car. Stroll on!" he exclaimed. "Why is it always me that cops it? I can't just capture any common-or-garden horrible hairy monster, me! I've got to bring in one that's covered in duck-dirt!"

Conversation lapsed as the police car cruised on. Keeping at a safe distance so as not to be observed, the Ford Escort continued to follow the police car through the London streets.

Leaving the hustle and bustle of the Saturday afternoon traffic behind, they had travelled up the Strand, along Fleet Street, past St Paul's Cathedral and then through the tall office blocks and skyscraper buildings of the City.

"How much further do you think they're taking him?" asked Henry.

"I don't know, lad," said Mr Perkins, adding stoutly, "But I do know this much, wherever they go – so do we!"

8

Albert Hollins's feet barely seemed to touch the ground as he was hustled along the white-walled corridor by Detective-Sergeant Cooney with Detective-Constable Poole close behind.

"In you go, my lad!" snapped Cooney, pushing Albert through the open door of a cell. "And you can stay in there until you're ready to give us your name and address. You play ball with us and we'll play ball with you. Isn't that so, Poole?"

The detective-constable scratched his head. Do you mean like *football*, Sarge?" he asked. "Or ping-pong?"

"No, you great soft silly wazzock!" snorted Cooney. "Never mind, lad – lock him up!"

Poole turned the iron key in the door and, for added safety, slammed home the big iron bolts.

Cooney nodded his approval. "And you'll remain on watch outside this door, Constable, until I tell you otherwise. Is that clear?"

"Yes, Sarge."

"And be advised by me, lad," warned the detective-sergeant, "don't fall for any of his, 'Please, Constable, can I make one phone call', or 'Please, Constable, can I use your lavvy' mullarkey – 'cos they're cunning blighters these monster-herberts, believe you me – I've come across them before."

"Have you, Sarge?" asked Detective-Constable Poole. "When was that then?"

Cooney shrugged his shoulders in some slight embarrassment. He was not exactly telling the truth. "Well, I've not come across one *personally*, Pooley," he admitted. "But I've *read* about 'em, in books and that. *And* I've seen 'em in late-night horror films on the telly. I'm here to tell you, Constable, that they not only possess the strength of ten men when they're roused – they're as fly as a barrow-load of monkeys to boot! Savvy?"

"I'm with you, Sarge."

"Good," said Cooney with satisfaction. Then, nodding his head towards the cell, he added, "That door is opened when I say it's opened, and not before."

"Right, Sarge. What do you think he's—"

"Sssshhhh!" went Cooney, putting a finger to his lips. "Listen! Can you hear anything?"

Poole put his head on one side, pressed an ear

to the cell door and listened carefully for several seconds. "Not a thing," he said at last.

"No, neither can I," mused the detective-sergeant. "He's a bit too quiet for my liking is our hairy friend. Just look through the peep-hole, Poole, and see what he's getting up to."

Poole put one eye to the hole in the door and peered inside. "Nothing, Sarge," he said.

"*Nothing*?"

"No, Sarge. Not a thing."

"Nothing at all?" asked Cooney, disbelievingly. "Do you mean to tell me he's *not* digging a tunnel with a sharpened teaspoon or tapping out a message to a fellow prisoner in an adjacent cell?"

Detective-Constable Poole shook his head. "He's not doing anything, Sergeant," he said. "He's just sitting there, on his bunk, with his hairy face buried in his hairy hands."

"Ah!" said Cooney, nodding his head knowledge-ably. "He'll be feeling sorry for himself then. The enormity of his past misdeeds will have suddenly overtaken him in his solitude. He'll be reflecting on his dreadful crimes and his misdemeanours. All right, Poole. He's all yours."

"Very good, Sarge," replied the constable.

"But just remember what I've said," warned Cooney. "Don't open the door to him. I shan't be far away. Just yell out if you want me. I shall be somewhere in the station – going about my official business."

"Yes," murmured Poole under his breath as Cooney strode off along the corridor, "I bet I know where that official business will take you, too – not far from the station canteen, I shouldn't wonder." Detective-Constable Poole sighed. The enticing smell of meat pie and chips was wafting up from the canteen at that very moment. He had not had anything to eat since breakfast – apart from a couple of Cooney's toffees, nutty ones – and the detective-sergeant had only given them to him because he didn't like the nutty ones himself. Poole wasn't over-fond of nutty toffees either. "What a rotten swizz!" he grumbled to himself.

"What a rotten swizz!" croaked Albert Hollins, taking his hairy head out of his hairy hands and glancing around the cold, bare, uninviting walls of his cell. "If this is what they call a holiday, give me the garden gnome factory in the middle of the Christmas rush! Diamond-Days Weekend indeed! I knew there'd be trouble from the moment that Emily suggested having a holiday – there always is. What was it we were promised? 'Two nights in the first-class hotel of our choice with tea-making facilities and en suite bathroom or shower.' And look what *I* end up with: an afternoon in a cop-shop cell with no bog, no bed, and not so much as a glass of water—"

Albert Hollins got to his feet and hammered on the door with his fists.

"Hey!" he called. "Is there anybody out there?"

"Worrisit?" Detective-Constable Poole's muffled voice called back.

"What chance is there of a cup of tea?"

"Flippin' no chance!"

"Can I use your lavvy then?"

"Naff off!" shouted Poole, remembering his sergeant's warning words about not letting the prisoner out under *any* circumstances.

"How about a telephone call? I'm entitled to make one phone call."

"You're entitled to nothing, matey!"

"Yes, I am!" croaked Albert, desperately. "I'm definitely entitled to a telephone call. I've seen them do it in these police series on the telly."

"When?"

"Many a time."

"Name one then."

"Name one what?"

"Name me a police series where you've seen a prisoner make a telephone call."

"All the time!" croaked Albert through the cell door. "Whenever anybody gets arrested. They always let them make a phone call to their lawyers."

"Not *monsters* they don't, chum!" replied Poole triumphantly. "*Ordinary* prisoners – yes. But never monsters. Monsters don't have lawyers. You never saw Dracula phone his lawyer, did you? You've never heard of Frankenstein ringing up a solicitor. Or the werewolf. Go on – you tell me when you last saw the werewolf pick up a phone and dial his lawyer's number!"

Albert Hollins did not reply. What would be the use? The constable outside the door of his cell was absolutely right. Monsters did not call up lawyers on the telephone. So what could he do with a phone call even if he *was* allowed to make one? There wasn't anyone that he could ring. Certainly not Emily – she must not be allowed to find out that he had turned into a horrible hairy monster. She'd go raving bonkers. And, if not Emily, who else could he turn to? There was always Henry, of course. But he hadn't got the first idea where Henry was.

Albert Hollins slumped back on to his bunk, defeated and downcast, and sank his head into his hands again. Although he was not aware of it, Henry was at that very moment standing by to help.

Henry Hollins and Mr Perkins had followed close behind the police car, so when it eventually pulled up, and Albert Hollins had been bundled into the police station, Reggie Perkins had parked his own car some twenty metres or so away on the opposite side of the street. They had been waiting anxiously inside the Escort ever since – unable, it seemed, to offer any assistance to the unfortunate Albert Hollins.

"Isn't there anything we can do, Mr Perkins?" asked Henry for the umpteenth time.

The hotel porter solemnly shook his head. "Not a lot, young Hollins," he replied, "except bide our time."

"But it's over half an hour since they took Dad inside," said Henry, his eyes fixed firmly on the police-station door. "When do you think they'll let him out again?"

"When they've finished with him, lad, and not a minute before," said Perkins, giving a hopeless little shrug. "They'll turn him loose, Henry, as soon as they've completed their enquiries – you can be sure of that."

"Enquiries into what, though?" asked Henry. "Dad hasn't done anything wrong."

"*I* know that and *you* know that, Henry, but the police don't know it," said Perkins. "Your father, Henry Hollins, is a poor unfortunate creature of circumstance. He's had the sheer bad luck to get himself turned into that foul fiend, Edward Hyde. You can't entirely blame the forces of law and order for taking *some* sort of interest in him – especially when your dad's had the downright misfortune to get himself apprehended trespassing on a little island in St James's Park that's normally considered the private domain of royal ducks."

"But it could have happened to anybody," said Henry.

"Precisely so – only unfortunately cruel fate has decreed that it shall happen to your dad." Perkins paused and looked hard into Henry's face before continuing, "Are you positive, lad, that we shouldn't advise your mum as to your dad's whereabouts?"

Henry Hollins nodded firmly. "I'm sure of that," he said.

"But she must be wondering where you are, the pair of you. She must be absolutely worried stiff!"

"I know," said Henry, in a small sad voice.

"I'm absolutely worried stiff," said Emily Hollins as she reached for the sugar bowl. "One lump or two?"

"No sugar for me, thanks, Mrs Hollins," replied Debbie, as she patted her stomach. "I'm watching my figure."

The two ladies were taking afternoon tea in the Hotel Emilion's Street-Sellers of Old London Coffee Shop. They were sitting underneath a mural depicting a bare-footed waif selling bunches of lavender, and the waitress had just served them with a pot of tea for two, some egg-and-cress sandwiches and a mouth-watering selection of cream cakes.

"I'm at my wits' end, Debbie, I really am," sighed Emily, handing her a cup of tea. "What do you think I should do, Debbie? What would *you* do if you were me?"

Debbie shook her head as she selected an egg-and-cress sandwich. "I haven't got the faintest idea, Mrs Hollins," she said.

"Well – what's done is done, I suppose," said Emily, "but I'm by no means sure that I've done what's best." As she spoke, she slipped a man's tie out of its slim pasteboard container and held it up for Debbie's inspection. "You see, I've bought this green one with the red spots – but looking at it again, in this light, I'm not sure that I wouldn't have been wiser to have got the brown one with the little squiggly yellow diamonds all over it. I could take it back and change it, I suppose. What's your opinion?"

"Don't ask me, Mrs Hollins," said Debbie. "It's hard to tell with ties – you can't say whether they'd suit or not if you aren't acquainted with the gentleman they're intended for."

"I bought it for Mr Wormald – Albert's boss at the garden gnome factory where he works," explained Emily. "Mr Wormald is a tall distinguished gentleman with a little moustache. He goes in a lot for caravanning – he's got his own permanent caravan on a camp site near Filey. Do you think a green tie with red spots would go down well in an East Coast holiday resort?"

"I don't see why not," said Debbie, eyeing the cream cakes. "It's always a problem isn't it, buying people presents when you come down to London?" As she spoke, she took a little black box out of her handbag, opened it, removed the contents and handed them to Emily. "I've bought my dad these left-handed toenail clippers – but I'm not sure that I've done the right thing, not with his toes."

Emily Hollins turned the shiny bright toenail clippers over in her hands. "Oh, they're *very* nice! They *are* nice! *Very* distinctive! You *are* clever, Debbie," she said, enviously. "I'd never have thought of buying Mr Wormald a pair of toenail clippers; never in a million trillion years!"

"Thank you," said Debbie, modestly, as she slipped the clippers back inside their box. "I think that green and red tie is lovely, as a matter of fact. I'm sure that Mr Wormald will like it. Why don't you ask your husband his opinion?"

"Oh, *him*!" sighed Emily, despairingly. "He's hopeless on ties, is Albert. You should have seen the purple monstrosity he'd have worn to the Garden Gnomes Limited's Annual Dinner and Dance and Sales Representative of the Year Awards – if I hadn't put the kybosh on him wearing it." Emily paused and frowned. "In any case," she continued in puzzled tones, "I don't know where he is to ask him – I haven't set eyes on either Albert or Henry all afternoon."

"They'll be out sightseeing, I bet," said Debbie.

"It's all very well for some," said Emily. "But a fat lot of sightseeing I look like doing if they don't turn up soon. We're going home tomorrow."

"Hey!" announced Debbie, excitedly. "Do you feel like doing some sightseeing now?"

"With you?"

Debbie nodded. "Why not?" she said. "I've done all the shopping I'm going to do on this trip. It's only half past four. We could whizz round London, see all the sights, and still be back here at the hotel in time for your Diamond-Days Weekend three-course candle-lit dinner inclusive of coffee and after-dinner mints in the hotel's Windsor Room Late-Nite Restaurant."

"I wouldn't say 'no'," said Emily. "But how could we manage a trip round London? It'd cost an absolute fortune to take a cab."

"It won't cost us anything at all, Mrs Hollins," said the hostess, looking round the coffee shop. "Do you see that gentleman sitting over there?"

Emily peered across the room. "Do you mean the bald-headed chap with the glasses?" she asked. "The one in the dark grey suit reading the *Financial Times* and sucking an orange?"

"That's him," said Debbie. "That's Leo Sopwith – he's the chauffeur to an Arab prince who's staying in this hotel."

Emily's eyebrows shot up. "My word!" she said, very impressed.

"I was chatting to him earlier on. Prince Achmed's given him the day off. He'll chauffeur us around – he loves a drive and the Prince doesn't mind at all if Leo borrows the coach."

"An Arab prince's coach, no less!" gasped Emily. "Is it like the coronation coach with six white horses?"

"It's more of a motor-coach actually," explained Debbie. "You see, the Prince has got these fifty wives. But it's a fully-fitted custom-built job. It's got little table-lamps throughout and a hot-drinks dispenser at the back. So what do you say then, Mrs Hollins? Do you fancy it?"

"I'll say!" said Emily, eagerly. "Albert and Henry will be green with envy when they hear that I've been cruising round London in a prince's coach!"

"Come on," said Debbie, getting to her feet and giving Leo Sopwith a sunny smile across the coffee shop.

"Oh!" said Albert Hollins sharply as a strange and

curious feeling passed through his entire body. "Oooooh!" he went as another mysterious tremor, stronger this time, shook him from head to foot. "Aaaaaaahhh!" he cried as the extraordinary sensation engulfed him again. "Oh, my goodness me!" he said as he sat down heavily on the cell bunk.

Mr Hollins sat upright and quite still, breathing heavily. Several seconds went by before he looked down and realized that a wonderful change had taken place. "They've gone!" he cried with delight. "All those hairs on the back of my hands! And . . . and my voice – it's *mine* again! I'm not croaking like Mr Hyde any longer!"

Hardly daring to believe his good fortune, Albert Hollins put his trembling hands up to his face. He was overjoyed to discover that his cheeks were smooth and hairless.

It really *was* true then!

Whatever transformation had overtaken him before, the effects of it had now worn off. No longer was he the horrible hairy Edward Hyde. He was good old Albert Hollins once more.

Getting to his feet, Mr Hollins banged again with his fists on the cell door. "Hey! You out there!" he yelled. "Let me out of here! Let me out of here at once!"

9

For several moments, Detective-Constable Poole tried to ignore the sounds that were coming from the monster's cell. But the hammering and shouting grew louder and in the end he was forced to reply.

"Hey, hey, hey!" he cried. "Less noise in there! It won't do you any good. You've been told already: there's no cups of tea for you, my lad, and there's no trips to the lavvy neither! I've had my orders. I've had very strict instructions from my senior officer. This door is staying very firmly shut until you're ready to reveal your true identity – to tell us who you are and where you come from!"

"I'm ready now," answered Mr Hollins from the other side of the door.

The news took the detective-constable completely by surprise. "Are you really?" he said.

"I've just said so, haven't I?"

"You're not kidding, by any chance? You're not trying to pull my leg?"

"No!"

It was true. Now that Mr Hollins was no longer a hairy horrible monster there was no reason for him to hide who he was from anybody. If asked, he would willingly have climbed to the top of a mountain and shouted out his identity to the whole world.

But Detective-Constable Poole was not aware of the change that had overtaken the prisoner. Consequently, he was still a little doubtful as to the monster's intentions.

"See this wet, see this dry, slit your throat if you tell a lie," said Poole, licking a forefinger and holding it up in the air.

"Yes!"

"Say it then!"

Inside the cell, Albert Hollins licked his own forefinger, held it up and repeated the solemn oath. "See this wet, see this dry," he said, "slit my throat if I tell a lie."

Detective-Constable Poole was satisfied at last. "Hang on," he said, "I'll open the door."

Poole drew back the metal bolts, turned the big key in the lock and threw open the door. The total stranger staring at him from inside the cell caused him to blink with surprise. "Who the heckers are you?" demanded Poole.

"I am Albert Hollins, I live at 'Woodview',

Nicholas Nickleby Close, Staplewood, and I am employed in the front office and packing department of Garden Gnomes Ltd," said Albert Hollins. "And in case you don't believe me, you can ring the factory now – my boss, Mr Wormald, will be there, even though it's Saturday afternoon – because we're just completing an important export order of garden gnomes to the Gulf States—"

"Just a minute, just a minute," broke in Detective-Constable Poole. "Not so fast. I'll come to you in a minute. It's the other chappie I'm concerned about – the horrible hairy monster."

"There isn't a horrible hairy monster," Albert Hollins tried to explain. "There's only me."

But Detective-Constable Poole refused to listen. "We'll soon see about that," he said coldly. "Stand aside while I take a look."

Obediently, Mr Hollins stepped outside to allow the detective-constable to go in and examine the cell. Poole had been well trained at his police college to search premises and buildings thoroughly.

His eyes swept round the four walls of the cell. There were not many places where a monster might hide – only two, in fact.

"That's odd!" said Poole, as he looked in the first hiding place – behind the door – and found nothing there. Then, "That's strange!" he continued as he got down on his hands and knees and examined the second possible hiding place – underneath the bed – and found nothing there either.

"That's torn it!" he added gloomily as he heard the cell door slam behind him. He leapt to his feet. It was Poole's turn to hammer on the door with his fists and yell loudly, "Let me out! Let me out of here!"

But there was no one outside to listen to his pleas.

Albert Hollins had snatched at opportunity, locked the door on the detective-constable and was already on his way along the white-walled corridor.

Nobody in the bustling police station paid the slightest attention to Albert Hollins as he strolled towards the main doors. Even Detective-Sergeant Cooney himself, on his way back from the canteen, did not give Mr Hollins a second glance. There was no reason why Cooney should connect the clean-shaven, respectable-looking gentleman with the ugly-looking brute he had flung into the cell not half an hour before.

Albert Hollins pushed open the swing doors of the police station and walked out to freedom.

"Mr Perkins!" cried Henry. "Look! It's Dad!"

"So it is, Henry!" exclaimed the hotel porter, looking at Mr Hollins, who was standing on the steps of the police station and drinking in the afternoon air.

"He's not horrible and hairy any longer either," said Henry happily. "He's changed back into plain ordinary old Dad again!"

"So he has – and a good job too!" said Perkins. "Give him a shout, Henry – let him know that we're here."

Henry Hollins wound down the car window. "Dad! It's us! We're over here!" he called across the road.

Albert Hollins's face lit up with surprised delight at the sight of his son. He trotted across the road as Henry leaned back and opened the rear door of the car.

"My goodness me!" said Mr Hollins as he clambered into the back seat. "Am I glad to see the pair of you again!"

"We've been out here waiting since they marched you in there, Dad," said Henry. "We were just beginning to get worried. We were wondering what had happened to you?"

"I'm wondering what *hasn't* happened to me," said Mr Hollins with a sigh. "I'm beginning to wonder what else *could* happen to me."

"It's all behind you now, Mr Hollins, take my word for it," said Perkins over his shoulder, cheerfully. "Now that you're back to being your old self again, you can settle back and enjoy what's left of your Diamond-Days Weekend. What's it to be? Your wish is my command. Where would you like me to drive you first?"

"Away from here for starters," said Albert Hollins as an anxious frown crossed his brow. He had just remembered the detective-constable he had locked inside the cell. "Before the word gets round that cop-shop that I've escaped – and they send the entire Flying Squad out to look for me."

"No sooner said than done," said Perkins. "I'll turn round further up the street and we'll head for the bright lights of the West End."

"Sightseeing here we come, Dad, eh?" said Henry.

Mr Hollins, in the back seat, smiled happily.

But in their joy at having put their problems behind them, the threesome in the Escort failed to notice the two men who had just come out of the police station and were now standing on the steps, looking up and down the road.

"Keep your eyes skinned, Poole," growled Cooney, who had released his detective-constable from the station cell. The two policemen had rushed outside to apprehend the villain who had perpetrated this crime. "What was he like, Pooley, the chap that overpowered you?" continued Cooney. "Big bloke, was he?"

Poole hesitated. He was not going to admit to Cooney that the man who had slammed the cell door shut on him was much smaller than himself. "*Very* big, Sarge," he said, putting a hand up high above his head. "About so big, I should think – and broad-shouldered with it too."

Cooney whistled through his teeth. "Crikey!" he gasped. "About six foot three, eh? It's a wonder nobody saw him walking into the station. The plot thickens, Poole. The monster has an accomplice. Well, they shouldn't be too difficult to spot – a horrible hairy monster and a big six-footer—" He broke off as the Escort, which had turned round further up the road, now sped past them on its way back into the West End.

"Hello!" snapped Cooney. "Did you see that?"

"What, Sarge?"

"That motor, lad! I'll swear it's that same Escort I

noticed on our tail when we drove out here from St James's Park. I'll bet that's them! Come on, Poole – after 'em!"

Detective-Sergeant Cooney, with the eager Poole at his heels, raced down the steps of the police station towards the vehicle which they had left parked up the road. Moments later, the police car had pulled away from the kerb and they were off in pursuit of their quarry.

Inside the Escort meanwhile, Albert, Henry and Perkins were relaxed and cheerful – unaware of the police car hot on their trail.

"Come along then!" said the hotel porter. "One of you make up your mind. Where's it to be? What would you like me to show you first? The Tower of London, perhaps? Marble Arch, maybe? An hour in the Natural History Museum before it closes?"

Albert thought hard and then shook his head. "I don't know," he said. "I can't think straight – this holiday's been like an awful nightmare up till now. You choose somewhere, Henry."

Henry Hollins did not need to give any thought to the matter. "You know what I would like to do most, Dad," he said. "Can we go to the Waxworks – Madame Tussaud's?"

"We could pop in there, I suppose," said Albert. "Always provided, of course, that Mr Perkins hasn't any objections?"

"None whatsoever," said the hotel porter. "I've been meaning to pay it a visit myself for some months past."

"We can't stay there long though," warned Mr Hollins. "We shall have to be getting back to the hotel soon, Henry, to put your mother's mind at rest."

With the decision taken, Perkins put his foot down on the accelerator and the Escort shot forward. Behind the Escort, the police car also picked up speed.

There was no way, Cooney told himself, that he was going to let the occupants of the car in front escape him yet again.

"I think it's lovely!" breathed Emily Hollins, her face pressed up against the railings outside the home of the Royal Family. "It's just like a palace!"

"It *is* a palace," Debbie pointed out. "It's Buckingham Palace."

"I know," said Emily, nodding happily. "And I'm glad I've stood outside it. I wouldn't like to live there though."

"Why ever not?"

"I wouldn't fancy having to pay the window-cleaner's bills," said Emily, frowning.

"We ought to be going soon," said Debbie, glancing at her watch. "We've been here fifteen minutes and Mr Sopwith has got the Prince's coach parked round the corner on a double yellow line."

Emily sighed and nodded. "I suppose we ought," she said. "And I should be getting back to the hotel to see if Albert and Henry have turned up yet. I've had such a lovely time, Debbie – it would be nice if we could manage just *one* more bit of sightseeing before we pack it in."

"Where had you in mind?" asked Debbie.

"Well . . ." began Emily thoughtfully, "a weekend in London wouldn't really seem complete without a trip to the Waxworks – Madame Tussaud's."

Debbie smiled. "Come on," she said. "I think we might just have time to nip over there and have a quick look round before they close the doors for the night."

"That's the car, Sarge – definitely," said Detective-Constable Poole, walking round the Escort which was parked in a side street off the bustling Euston Road.

"Are you absolutely sure, Poole?" growled Detective-Sergeant Cooney.

Poole nodded. "I recognize the nodding toy Alsation in the rear window," he said, "and the two big fluffy dice hanging in the front. Besides, I saw it turn left into this street."

"Then why the heckers didn't you turn left when

they did!" snapped Cooney. "Instead of driving two streets further on!"

"It wasn't my fault, Sarge," said Poole. "I didn't know they were going to turn off when they did. My left-hand indicator doesn't work – by the time I'd wound the window down to do my hand signal it was too late – we'd passed the turning. But this is the car all right, Sarge – I'm positive of it."

"And a fat lot of good that is to us!" continued Cooney angrily. "It's not the *car* we're after, Constable, it's the villains who were inside it." He looked up and down the street. "And *I* can't see anyone who looks anything like a horrible hairy monster *or* his six-foot-three accomplice. We've lost them again, Poole – thanks to you."

"We could wait here and trap them when they come back," suggested the detective-constable.

"Oh, yes?" said Cooney. "Brilliant! And supposing they *don't* come back? How long do you plan to hang around here then? For all you know, lad, they could have abandoned this vehicle – for good. For all you know, it could be stolen property. We could be hanging about for *yonks*!"

"We could go away for half an hour, Sarge," suggested Poole, "sort of have a look around and then come back again."

"Have a look round where?" asked Cooney, suspiciously.

"Have a look round there," replied Poole, pointing along the street.

Cooney looked across the Euston Road at the large inviting building to which Poole was pointing. "In *there*?" echoed Cooney, questioningly.

"It's the Waxworks, Sarge – it's Madame Tussaud's."

"I know the Waxworks when I see it, Poole," snapped Cooney. "But what cause have you and I got to pay Madame Tussaud's a visit? We're supposed to be on duty."

"It's brill in there!" Poole's voice rose excitedly. "Especially in the Chamber of Horrors – it's better than the Black Museum at New Scotland Yard. You can see these waxwork villains being hanged and electrocuted and having their heads chopped off and that. It's *really* brill! You'd like it!"

Detective-Sergeant Cooney stroked his chin. He had to admit to himself that the prospect *was* appealing. "I suppose we could pop in for a quick skeg round," he said, "and then come straight back here and see if there's any sign of that monster and his evil accomplice."

Poole chewed at his lower lip. "There's only one problem, Sarge," he said. "I'm a bit strapped for cash at the moment – can you lend me the price of the admission ticket?"

"Admission ticket?" repeated Cooney, shaking

his head pityingly. "We're members of the Metropolitan Police Force, Poole – we'll flash our warrant cards at the woman in the pay-box and say we're looking for a couple of suspects. Come on!"

As Detective-Sergeant Cooney and Detective-Constable Poole set off towards the entrance to the Waxworks, a gleaming motor coach cruised slowly into the side street looking for a parking place. There were two eager faces pressed to the coach's windows.

"There it is!" said Debbie. "Madame Tussaud's!"

"I'm really looking forward to it," said Emily Hollins.

"It's ace in here, Dad, isn't it?" said Henry Hollins, gazing round the Chamber of Horrors.

"It's . . . it's all right, I suppose," said Albert Hollins, none too surely.

"All right?" scoffed Henry. "It's better than all right, Dad – it's ace! *Great*! Don't you think that it's great in here, Mr Perkins?"

"I think that it's highly entertaining, Henry," said Perkins, nervously.

They had already looked at the waxwork man being hanged. They had seen the waxwork man being guillotined. They had stared at the waxwork man sitting in the electric chair. They were standing now at the end of a gloomy Victorian cobbled street where a waxwork Jack the Ripper hovered in a doorway while the body of one of his waxwork victims lay, brutally murdered, in a pool of blood in a gas-lit doorway. It was all rather creepy and bloodcurdling.

It was almost closing time at the Waxworks and Henry, Albert Hollins and Perkins, the hotel porter, were the only visitors left in the Chamber of Horrors.

Mr Hollins shivered, although it was quite warm. "You might find it highly entertaining, Mr Perkins," he said. "But I can think of other places I'd rather be in right now."

"I think it's really great, Dad!" exclaimed Henry, peering into the shadowy alleyways along the cobbled street. "I can just imagine a spooky monster hiding in every doorway!"

"Do you have to bring up the subject of monsters, Henry?" gulped Albert Hollins. The chilling atmosphere inside the Chamber of Horrors was having an unfortunate effect on poor Mr Hollins.

"Ooooh-er!" he groaned, as a strange but not entirely unfamiliar sensation passed through his entire body. He began to tremble violently. It was happening to him again.

"Are you all right, Dad?" asked Henry, anxiously.

"Oh!" and "Aaaaaagghhh!" cried Albert Hollins.

"What is it, Mr Hollins?" said Perkins in some concern.

"Brrrrrr!" went Albert Hollins as another spasm shook him all over.

Dark hairs had begun to sprout again all over his face, and his cheeks and forehead were growing wrinkled and leathery.

"I think it's my fault, Dad," said Henry. "I don't think I should have brought you into the Chamber of Horrors – you're turning back into Mr Hyde again."

Albert Hollins let out a long, hollow sigh as he stared down at the black hair which had suddenly covered the back of his hands. "I thought I'd finished with all of this," he croaked.

"At least you know that it's going to wear off, Dad," said Henry, trying to comfort his poor father. "And perhaps it won't last as long this time."

"We'll have to do something about it *now*, though," said Perkins. "There's somebody coming. You'd better hide."

"Where?" groaned Albert, glancing round the room.

"Quick, Dad! Over here!" said Henry. "I've got an idea—"

"What do you think of it so far, Sarge?" asked Detective-Constable Poole as he led the way through the Chamber of Horrors.

Detective-Sergeant Cooney gave a nervous little cough. He hadn't realized when he agreed to come that it would be *quite* so spine-chilling. "Not bad, Poole," he replied, trying to conceal his fears. "Not bad at all."

"Hey – look over there, Sarge!" said Poole excitedly, as they rounded a corner. "There's an old-fashioned street with some gas lamps in it and a waxwork murder. Let's take a closer look."

Cooney was a little relieved to discover that at least they were not alone in the Chamber of Horrors. "Good evening!" he said to the man and the boy who were standing looking down the cobbled street.

Henry Hollins and Perkins exchanged an anxious glance. They had recognized the newcomers as the two policemen who had arrested Albert earlier that day.

"G-g-g-good evening," stammered Perkins.

"Hello," gulped Henry.

But there was no reason why Cooney and his detective-constable should know who Henry Hollins and Perkins were – in any case, they were more interested in the sinister Victorian street and its waxwork figures than in the Waxworks' human customers.

"Golly Moses!" enthused Poole, staring into the street. "Just look at all that *blood*, Sarge, where it's dripped on the pavement off that waxwork body – doesn't it look real! Do you think that's a waxwork Jack the Ripper peeping round that corner?"

But Detective-Sergeant Cooney was peering hard at another figure in the waxwork tableau. "Take a look at that one, Poole," he said, pointing into one of the shadowy doorways. "Doesn't it remind you of someone?"

The detective-constable screwed up his eyes and looked. The figure in question was hairy and horrible. "Hey! You're right, Sarge! It looks just like that monster we nicked in St James's Park!"

Albert Hollins, crouching in the doorway, did his very best not to move a muscle – even though he was inwardly quaking with fear.

"It's a waxwork Mr Hyde," said Henry Hollins, whose idea it had been for his father to pose as one of the exhibits.

"You know," added Perkins, "the chap that changed from Doctor Jekyll after swallowing some of that mixture he'd invented."

"Ooooh, yes!" said Poole. "So it is! I remember seeing the movie on the telly, Sarge."

But Cooney was not as easily fooled as his young and less experienced detective-constable. He continued to keep his gaze fixed on the crouching figure in the doorway.

"Hello, hello, hello!" he said at last. "It blinked."

"It can't have blinked," said Henry. "It's a waxwork."

"It blinked, I tell you!" snorted Cooney. "It's just done it again."

"Do you know, I think you're right, Sarge," said Poole. "I saw it that time."

"We're going to investigate this," said Cooney, stepping over the knee-high red rope that divided the waxwork tableau from the public area. "Come on, Constable!"

10

"Come *on*, Poole!" repeated Cooney, beckoning impatiently to his detective-constable on the other side of the red rope.

Poole shook his head. "I don't think we're supposed to cross over that rope, Sergeant," he said.

"Don't be a wally, Poole!" snapped the detective-sergeant. "We're detectives – we can go wherever we please!"

"Oh no, you can't!" cried a warning voice.

The tall man who had just entered the Chamber of Horrors was dressed in the uniform of an attendant. His name was Leonard Grimshaw and he was on his way round the building informing the visitors that the Waxworks would shortly be closing down for the night. He was astonished to discover that a member of the public had climbed over into one of the exhibition tableaux.

"Come along, sir," said Grimshaw quietly. "You're not allowed in there, you know."

Cooney pulled himself up to his full height. "I am Detective-Sergeant Leslie Cooney," he said, "and it is my intention to inspect and possibly apprehend that horrible hairy monster over there!"

"And I am Attendant Grimshaw, sir, and it's my duty to advise you that members of the paying public are not allowed to touch the exhibits."

"He's not even a *paying* member of the public, Leo." The voice had come from a second uniformed attendant who, hearing raised voices, had come down into the Chamber of Horrors to find out what the fuss was about. "He didn't cough up so much as a penny to come inside," continued the newcomer whose name was Horace Agthorpe. "I saw him waving his arms about and shouting at Peggy in the pay-box not long ago."

"I only told her what I'm telling you," snapped Cooney. "That I've come in here in pursuit of a couple of missing villains: a horrible hairy monster and his six-foot-three accomplice. I have good reason to believe that the horrible hairy monster is crouching in that doorway over there."

The two attendants looked along the dimly lit cobbled street to where the detective-sergeant was pointing. They had neither of them seen the crouching figure before – but then, the waxwork figures were constantly being added to and changed inside the exhibition. And, judging by its hairy and horrible appearance, there was no doubt that the crouching figure in the doorway *was* a waxwork – there was no way that it could possibly be a living person.

It was not difficult to guess, either, what it was supposed to represent.

"That is quite plainly a waxwork model, sir, of that well-known Victorian rascal, Edward Hyde – of Doctor Jekyll and Mr Hyde fame," said Attendant Grimshaw. "Wouldn't you say so, Horace?"

"Most definitely," agreed Attendant Agthorpe. "It couldn't possibly be anything else. Now then, sir, we must ask you to step back over that red rope this instant!"

Cooney looked at the two attendants and then at the monster crouching in the doorway. He decided that he had to finish what he had started to do.

The detective-sergeant moved quickly – but the two attendants moved quicker still. Before Cooney had taken two steps towards the monster, Grimshaw and Agthorpe had leapt over the red rope and taken firm hold of him.

"I'm sorry to have to do this, sir," said Leonard Grimshaw, "but those waxwork figures are very valuable – rules do have to be obeyed."

"We must ask you to accompany us to the manager's office," said Agthorpe. "You can explain to him what all this is about."

"I've already told you what it's all about," moaned Cooney, struggling in the grip of the two attendants. "I'm a detective-sergeant – that's my detective-constable standing over there. *You* tell them what we're doing here, Poole."

But Poole had not approved of Cooney's decision to cross the red rope in the first place. He shrugged his shoulders now and grinned apologetically at Grimshaw and Agthorpe.

As Detective-Sergeant Cooney was led away protesting loudly, Detective-Constable Poole fell in behind and followed in their wake.

Albert Hollins let out a croak of relief. He had been crouching motionless for several minutes. "Thank goodness they've gone," he groaned, stretching his aching muscles. "I've got pins and needles all down my back!"

"You can't move yet, Dad!" said Henry, warningly. "Somebody else is coming!"

"Oh, no!" sighed Albert Hollins as he took up his crouching position in the shadowy doorway again. "What now?"

"Our Henry!" gasped Emily Hollins, rounding a corner in the Chamber of Horrors. "Fancy bumping into you in here of all places!"

"Hello, Mum," said Henry Hollins.

"Why, if it isn't Mr Perkins too!" said Debbie, close on Emily's heels.

"Greetings, Deborah," said the hotel porter. "Surprise, surprise! What a pleasant coincidence! What brings you to the Chamber of Horrors?"

"The same reason that brought you two here, I suppose," said Debbie. "We're sightseeing."

"But why aren't you with your father, Henry—" Emily Hollins broke off and her mouth fell open with surprise as she glanced along the cobbled street. "Albert Hollins!" she cried. "Whatever do you think you're doing in that exhibit? Come back here before you get yourself into hot water!"

"That's funny!" said Albert Hollins to himself as he remained stock still, crouching in the doorway. "How the dickens did she recognize me . . ."

Without moving his head, he allowed his eyes to stray down to his hands. The thick black hair was gone. He felt his cheeks and chin. They were smooth and hairless. Without even knowing, he had changed back into himself again. His second spell as horrible hairy Edward Hyde had lasted no more than a few minutes.

The effects of the mixture were finally wearing off for good. It was more than likely, he felt sure, that he would never become horrible and hairy again.

Albert Hollins smiled a contented smile.

Henry Hollins and Perkins, realizing what had happened, smiled at each other.

168

"And why on earth were you crouching down like that?" asked Emily, as Albert came along the cobbled street towards her. "You're not *still* having trouble with your back, I hope? I thought that doctor had given you something for it. Do you think you ought to go back and see him again?"

"No, Emily," said Albert, firmly shaking his head as he climbed back over the red rope. "No, I don't. Most definitely not."

Suddenly, the Chamber of Horrors was full of chattering voices as a tall Arab entered, followed by fifty ladies dressed in spotless white linen robes.

"Well, I'm blowed!" said Perkins. "Look who's here! It's the Hotel Emilion's VIP, Prince Achmed! Hello, Your Royal Highness – fancy bumping into you here!"

"Perkins, by all that is holy!" exclaimed the prince, clasping his hands together in front of his chest. "Truly it is written that the world is full of surprises."

"You've got your wives with you as well," said the hotel porter. "I thought they'd split up and gone off to see Windsor Castle or to watch West Ham play Tottenham Hotspurs?"

The smile faded from the prince's face as he slowly shook his head. "Alas, oh inestimable Perkins, the twenty-five of them who set out for Windsor Castle became quickly envious of the twenty-five at Upton Park – while the twenty-five at the football match were soon made disconsolate by an entire absence of goal-mouth incident. Both parties decided separately to come here instead – which is where I myself have spent the afternoon. But now the Waxworks is about to close and the taxis that they came in are scattered around the London streets as sand is blown by wind across the desert. In short, wise Perkins, I am abysmally lacking the transport to convey my ladies back to the hotel."

"No, you're not, Your Highness," said Debbie. "We've got your coach parked outside."

"We borrowed it to see the sights, Your Majesty," said Emily, doing a little curtsy. "I hope that was all right?"

It was plain from Prince Achmed's expression that he did not mind at all. He beamed down on Perkins, Debbie and the Hollins family. "Truly is it written that Allah is great and good and kind," he said. "And that round every corner is a silver lining. Come! You shall all be my guests! We shall see the sights of London together!"

"Hey! Look, Henry!" said Emily Hollins, pointing excitedly out of the window of the prince's coach. "There's the Houses of Parliament!"

The coach was cruising over Westminster Bridge.

"And there's Big Ben!" cried Mr Hollins.

Emily leant back happily in her comfortable seat. "I'll bet there aren't many folk in Stapleford that can say they've been all round London in a real live prince's coach – with the prince himself *and* all his wives," she said.

"Not a lot, I fancy," agreed Albert.

"Well, all things considered," continued Emily, "I think it's turned out very well, our Diamond-Days Weekend – what do you say, Henry?"

"I think it's turned out ace, Mum," replied Henry Hollins. "T'riffic – brilliant!"

Albert Hollins did not feel disposed to argue with them.

Debbie moved along the aisle of the coach feeling quite at home. "I'll tell you what I'm going to do," she said. "I'm going to put my in-coach hostess's hat on – metaphorically speaking. I'm going to get a sing-song going! Come on, Your Highness, come on your Royal Ladyships – let's hear what kind of singing voices you've all got! All together now – Pack up your troubles! – one, two, three . . ."

As the luxury coach sped smoothly on towards Trafalgar Square, Henry Hollins, Emily Hollins, Albert Hollins, Perkins the hotel porter, Prince Achmed and his fifty wives all raised their voices in hearty song:

"Pack up your troubles in your old kit-bag
And smile, smile, smile . . ."

It was late evening several days later. The Hollinses were safely back at home in Staplewood. A lone blue-uniformed policeman was patrolling his beat around the many back streets behind the Hotel Emilion. He was feeling bad tempered. He had been on his feet all day and his brand new boots

172

were tight and pinched his toes. He frowned as he spotted a man in a raincoat peering round the corner of an alleyway.

The uniformed policeman tiptoed up behind the man in the raincoat and tapped him on the shoulder. "Hello, hello, hello!" he said. "What's your game, my lad?" The man in the raincoat turned and the policeman's eyebrows shot up in surprise. "Why!" he continued. "It's Constable Stiggins, isn't it? What are you doing out of uniform?"

"I'm not plain Constable Stiggins any longer," said Timothy Stiggins proudly. "I've been promoted. I'm Detective-Constable Stiggins now. But what are you doing *in* uniform? It is Detective-Sergeant Cooney, isn't it?"

Leslie Cooney gave a sad sigh and shook his head. "I've been *de*moted," he said. "I've been put back on the beat. I'm not Detective-Sergeant Cooney any longer – I'm just plain Constable Cooney now."

"Why's that?" asked Stiggins in astonishment. "What happened?"

"It's a long story," said Cooney. The truth of the matter was that his superior officers had not approved of his peculiar behaviour in the Chamber of Horrors. Detective-sergeants, in their opinion, did not go messing about with waxwork figures and climbing over red ropes into parts of exhibitions where they were not supposed to go. But Cooney did not want to pursue that subject now. "Why were you looking into this alleyway?" he asked.

Stiggins smiled mysteriously. "Come with me," he said, beckoning Cooney to follow him. "I'll show you something rather exciting!"

Stiggins led the way along the alley and Cooney limped after him. They came out into a curious cobbled square. It was a strange place, with an eerie flickering gas lamp casting shadows into odd corners. It reminded Cooney of the spooky Victorian street in the Chamber of Horrors.

"See there?" said Stiggins, pointing up into the topmost branches of one of the two gnarled trees set in the cobblestones. "There's an owl lives in that tree!"

Promotion, it seemed, had not diminished Timothy Stiggins' love of bird-watching.

"Don't be daft," growled Cooney. "There aren't any owls in central London."

"There's one up there," repeated Stiggins, firmly. "I've heard it."

Their conversation was interrupted by the sound of footsteps.

Doctor Henry Jekyll was returning home, clutching a slip of paper tightly in one hand. It was his great-grandfather's formula. He had just managed to get it back from the chemist's shop. It had been very careless, he told himself, to allow that poor

Mr Hollins to go off with it. He hoped he had not caused his patient any problems. He would have to lock it away safely when he got back indoors. If he could remember, that is . . . He was getting so forgetful of late . . .

"Good evening, sir!" said Detective-Constable Stiggins as the old gentleman drew near.

"Good evening to you too," said Doctor Jekyll as he passed the two men.

"Ouch!" groaned Constable Cooney.

"Is something the matter?" asked the old doctor.

"It's my feet," said Cooney. "These boots are brand new and they're killing me!"

"Oh dear me!" said Henry Jekyll, sympathetically. "Why don't you step into my surgery and let me have a look – I may be able to give you something for that." He pointed to the old dark door set in the tall gloomy building in the farthest corner of the square. "My name is Doctor Henry Jekyll," he added.

"Thanks very much!" said Cooney eagerly. "I'll take you up on that, Doctor."

"Do you think it's safe to go with him?" whispered Stiggins as the old gentleman set off across the yard. "His name is Doctor Jekyll, after all!"

"Of course it's safe, you wally!" snapped Cooney. "He's only going to give me a prescription – what possible harm could come from that? So long, Stiggins – I'll see you around."

Moments later, the old dark door had closed behind Doctor Jekyll and Constable Cooney.

Detective-Constable Timothy Stiggins was left standing all alone in the cobbled yard.

It was beginning to get quite dark and there was just a hint of swirling fog. The branches of the gnarled trees were heavy with leaves that hung motionless in the still air.

"Whoo-hooooo*oooh*!" went the wise old owl.